T5-AFS-899

Beige

a novella in three acts

By

Grant Kuchan

Copyright © 2012 by Grant Kuchan

Cover Photo Copyright © 2012 by Grant Kuchan

All rights reserved. No portion of this book may be
reproduced, except for review purposes, without written
permission of the copyright holder.

This is a highly satirical work of fiction. All characters,
organizations, or events portrayed in this novella are either
invented by the author or used fictitiously.

Special Thanks:
Gabriel, Mr. Redpen, and, of course, Ali

This book is dedicated to the 10 people who purchased my
first book. This is all your fault.

ISBN # 978-0-9840293-2-7

Act One:

Harold and His Truth

Stabbing

When observed from the outside, scientists theorize that the universe has a beige hue.

Scientists also theorize that the average temperature of the universe is 2.73 degrees above absolute zero.

This is the universe attempting to find balance.

This is the universe striving toward mediocrity.

This is a story about cold, average people, who really found beige shockingly pedestrian. This, like all stories could begin anywhere, or at anytime.

That is the wonderful thing about telling a story. There is no "right" place to start. Even once the author chooses, as happens with people in real life, we can play along the time line of these creations.

People are mistaken in thinking that they live their lives in a linear fashion. People live their lives with a constant attachment to both their past and their future. People are constantly looking at their present situations, through the veil of everything that has happened before, and everything that they hope to come.

People also wander through their lives believing that their favorite color is yellow. Everyone's favorite color is beige.

Except for Horace. Horace is the exception to this rule. This is ironic, because Horace is a Semi-colon.

The typical Semi-Colon, when observed in its natural habitat, is a rather unassuming, but necessary, fellow. Often, when used correctly within a sentence, with a grace unique unto itself, it will keep a sentence aloft; never asking for any praise, or thanks. On the QWERTY keyboard, it sits with its cousin the colon, quietly waiting for the writer to make that beautiful choice; abandoning more mundane punctuation for the Semi-Colon.

Horace however was not a typical Semi-Colon. Horace was, to be frank, at this very moment a very pissed off Semi-Colon. Something, which the large amounts of alcohol that Horace was intending to consume at the hotel bar, was not going to help.

The bar at the Holidaze Inn, when the hotel was initially built in the seventies, had been a testament to the bizarre love of psychedellia that the owners held. They felt that if they assisted in the freeing of the minds of the clientele; the world would eventually become a better place. Today, the hopelessly dated walls looked like an album cover had vomited on a piece of modern art. There were orange paisleys and brown mouths, which sat there smiling, and occasionally sticking out their tongues. If Horace had felt like it, he could have spent a good hour and a half mocking the place, the color scheme, the cheap lighting. But, after being discarded from the latest Chicago Manual of Style on the grounds of seeming esoteric; Horace was really more interested in getting drunk.

Very little official study has been done on the drinking habits of punctuation marks. One might suspect the exclamation point, or possibly even the introspective question mark to be the drinker in the crowd. Few have even suggested that it is actually the comma with its unyielding habit of being able to add more, and more, and yet even more, on. But, it is the Semi-colon that has been rumored as the heaviest drinker of all the punctuation marks; and Horace did little to dispel the myth. After being removed from an abridged version of The Dubliners, Horace went on a bender, causing him to miss the Harlem Renaissance as well as, mercifully, the majority of the Beats. Waking only to find him in the waning days of the golden age of science fiction, tucked into Omnibus of Robert Heinlein short stories.

A man in a grey suit sat at the other end of the bar. He was busy being marketed to, while watching millionaires play a game he used to play in high school. His history with the marketing campaign, which some people had labeled a "sport", coupled with a generous amount of alcohol boosted his ego and quickly turned him into what is commonly referred to as an "asshole".

The name of the man in the grey suit is unimportant. In the next few pages Horace will stab him repeatedly, and he will not reappear until the next chapter. Your only recollection will be that he is the guy whom Horace stabs in the beginning of this novella. But, for those of you who are keeping score his name is Harold Winestock. And he is just about to realize that he is sharing the bar with a punctuation mark.

Horace could feel the man in the grey suit staring at him. This was not an uncommon occurrence for Horace. Often people would stare and attempt to remember their elementary school grammar; hopelessly searching for the name of the strange being before them. When Horace was feeling generous, or just tired of being stared at, he would help.

"Semicolon," said Horace.

"What?" responded the grey suit.

"I'm a semicolon," said Horace.

"No, you aren't," slurred the grey suit.

Horace returned to his drink.

"Aren't you going to ask?" continued the grey suit.

"Ask what?"

"What I think you are."

"You'll have to excuse, me," said Horace. "I have been having a rough day. All I want is to relax with a drink. I really don't want to have to stab you."

"Whoa," said the grey suit. "How did we go from just talking to you stabbing me?"

"It's been a rough day," said Horace.

"Yeah, but people don't go from, 'hi' to 'I'll stab you'."

"I told you I'm a semicolon."

"Yeah, but that's not what you are," said the grey suit.

"Great," said Horace. "So, tell me how many other steps do we need to go through until I get to stab you?"

"I'm not really certain," said the grey suit.

"Really?" said Horace. "You sounded so sure of yourself; as if there were some kind of code as to the stages of your typical stabbing."

"Look why don't you just ask me what I think you are," said the grey suit.

"No, you're the one who brought it up so tell me," said Horace. "What are the stages to your typical stabbing?"

"I told you I don't know!"

"It happens in two stages," said Horace. "One minute you're not stabbed then next minute you are. Funny how that works, isn't it."

"I just wanted to say that you were the reason that I flunked freshman English," said the man in the grey suit. "I've never met a punctuation mark before."

"I'm the reason that you failed freshman English?" said Horace.

The tiny, bored bartender tore his eyes away from the marketing campaign on the television. As he was scanning the bar to see if anyone needed a refill. Horace motioned, the bartender slowly began to prepare another drink.

"Yes it's your fault," said the man in the grey suit.

"Had nothing to do with going away to college, girls or drinking?" said Horace. "It had absolutely nothing to do with you being a fucking moron."

The bartender placed the drink in front of Horace. He did have a moment where he thought about getting involved in the argument. As soon as people began to drop the expletive "fuck", he knew things would begin to spiral out of control shortly. He visualized himself diffusing the situation with grace, and a good deal of wit, and then as a reward receiving a substantial tip from both of his customers. Sadly, the review of a disputed play returned his attention to the marketing campaign, and the man in the grey suit was forced to face his destiny alone.

Many people question the existence of fate and of destiny. The thought that anything within the realm of human experience not be free will makes the average person believe that they are merely an actor following a script pre-ordained to lead them to an unpleasant end. Instead, most believe in the clearly more sensible theory that there is a creator who set the world in motion, laid down some vague rules and left it to our own devices. Hoping, in vain, that we wouldn't act like a rampaging group of three year olds left unsupervised in a kitchen with an abundance of orange soda and art supplies.

Horace and the man in the grey suit stared at each other in a typical male ritual of attempting to establish which the Alpha male was. This was something, which the man in the grey suit, having grown up in an upper middle class setting was not used to doing. Horace, however being a punctuation mark had been around long enough to know when to look crazy and when to look batshit crazy. And right now he looked batshit crazy. Horace also knew that if he continued to look at the man in the grey suit like this, that in another minute he would be established as the alpha male. Unless the man in the grey suit was so completely detached and insulated from any form of visceral threat that he would continue to stare at him. Horace made note of the expanding waistline of the man in the grey suit, which was even more exaggerated against the orange paisley wallpaper behind him, and made a choice.

The Winestocks

To most people, Harold Winestock's life deeply resembled a Norman Rockwell painting. This, however, was not uncommon in the affluent north shore suburb in which Harold lived. It, like many of the small towns and villages just north of Chicago, could equally be described as quaint. But, Harold's had clung to an outdated ideal with such vehemence, that it looked like much of the idealized images of Norman Rockwell. Children on bikes raced up and down the street, with their dogs following close behind them. Little girls sat with dolls in their front yards, and dutiful moms kept a watchful eye on the neighborhood, as Dad would contemplate the lawn. The schools were exceptional, and the streets were clean and well maintained.

Harold, like many of the men on his block had begun the slow expansion that comes with middle age. His wife, Ami, was a fit tall blond. Harold Junior, or HoJo, excelled at the private academy, which he attended. For all intents and purposes Harold, along with his neighbors lived a very charmed existence. That was until a Semi-colon stabbed him.

"So he actually stabbed you?" said a strikingly average late middle-aged white man. He stood in his living room, his wife busy in the kitchen. He was proud to let everyone know that it was his living room, his wife, and his kitchen. Throughout the house his beige walls were placed very far apart.

At this point in human history a good deal of importance was placed on precisely how far apart your walls were. Through a series of complex mathematical formulae which led to a term referred to as "square footage". Square footage was one of the many ways that most affluent white people used to keep score. The richest of these people would hire decorators. Decorators are paid extraordinary sums of money to transform square footage into "Living Space". Ami specialized in the transfer of "Living Spaces" from one individual to another; she could be labeled a Real Estate broker. Truth be told, she could be labeled a great many things, but she had a deep affinity for tastefully elegant "Living Spaces". She spent a great deal of time perfecting these "Living Spaces". She could find the perfect placement for a leather chair with a tasteful Afghan draped upon it. A small occasional table with a newer, but not controversial book on it, preferably a Pulitzer Prize winner, but lately so many of them had been controversial; she would usually go with something recommended on daytime television. Yes, she was wonderful with spaces and things. It was people who presented a problem. Like her husband, who had just returned from a business trip with a stab wound.

"All he was trying to do was make conversation," said Ami.

"How was I to know he was going to take offense to me joking around," said Harold. "That was all I was doing. Joking around."

"I'm not all that familiar with the rules of grammar, but I thought that the Semi-colon did something other than stab loud mouth drunks," said the average white man.

"There is no need to call me a loud mouth drunk," said Harold, with a good deal of confidence. Average affluent white men rarely stabbed other average affluent white men.

"See how easy it is when we introduce an innocent alcoholic beverage into the conversation."

The shockingly average white man was actually mistaken. Alcohol has been the most vilified of all of the mind-altering substances. It is nothing more than the urine of a microscopic organism with a voracious appetite. Blaming alcohol for societal ills would make as much sense as standing in your bathroom screaming at the toilet bowl; blaming your recent excretion for your own personal failings. Sadly though, many people spend a good deal of time screaming at their toilet.

"If this were a simple act of inciting violence against another individual, I could tell you precisely that the punctuation mark was wrong, but as it is I don't quite recall many of the rules of grammar."

This, however, was a shockingly insightful statement. The average white man was of the half generation before Harold. Harold thought that he might be able to help him understand the Semi-colon. Harold being an active member of the Internet revolution, of which one of the many casualties had been punctuation and grammar, really hadn't even thought about a Semi-colon until seeing him in the hotel bar. This of course was not his fault, with increases in the speed of communication the necessity to be understood correctly the first time, had fallen by the wayside. There was a time when a letter, hand written, could take weeks or even months to reach the intended recipient. Then, one could expect to wait another couple of weeks or months to receive a reply. If the original letter were not accurate and clear, another letter would need to be sent, adding on another couple of months. However, with the advent of electronic communications, issues could be discussed and clarified remarkably quickly. Therefore, there was no longer any need to actually write with any specificity.

This was one of the many reasons why punctuation marks drank.

Harold's son's generation took the lack of specificity to a whole new level. HoJo was a member of an elite generation who never knew a world without electronic communication.

At this moment he was standing in front of large Queen Anne style house, which had some beautiful walls that Ami had been hoping to sell for a very long time. HoJo's thirteen years of hormones, fought desperately to burst out of his pudgy frame.

"Let's go HoJo," said the other bundle of hormones next to HoJo, as he played with his tablet. His name was James, and had been friends with HoJo since kindergarten.

"No, if Andrew posted to his Individuality™ page he saw her naked, then either he is lying, or we might actually be able to see her naked," HoJo physically quivered at the thought.

"You know it won't make a difference," said James. "You can't even buddy her on Individuality™."

"You don't have to stay you don't want to," said HoJo. HoJo had been working desperately on this plan since he had read what Andrew had seen. Andrew stated that he had seen the object of most of HoJo obsessions, the Holy Grail of images: Kelly McIntyre. Naked.

HoJo felt cheated. No matter what he had been doing, on his way home he would stop and gaze up at the Queen Anne, even if it was in the opposite direction. HoJo had deduced that Kelly's bedroom was in the front of the house, and maybe, if the gods were smiling down upon him, he might just catch a glimpse of Kelly. In the seven years he had been walking by Kelly's house he had only seen her a handful of times. James thought that HoJo's obsession with Kelly might be bordering on the unhealthy. Subsequently, James had embarked on a campaign for HoJo to actually speak to Kelly, hoping that once HoJo did, the allure might fade. In HoJo's defense, he had tried to talk to her since the third grade, but always became tongue-tied. However, tonight, if he could prove that Andrew was lying, he would look like the hero he knew she would respect. If not, he might just see her naked.

"You're the one who came and got me," said James. "You don't need to be a prick."

HoJo let out a heavy sigh. There was little he disliked more than having to deal with James when he was feeling overly or overtly hormonal. There was no reason for him to feel quite so sensitive. This was nothing less than free porn, and he was whining.

"I don't mean to be a prick," said HoJo. "But you don't make it very easy."

"I heard the poor bastard was managing a Popeye's," said the shockingly average white male. Harold smiled at his wife, who was stifling a scowl. Ami had never been very good at laughing, it always sounded forced and fake, as if her laughing freely would show some kind of lack of control.

She acted the same way when it came to her orgasms. The shockingly average white man's wife however, howled with abandon. Her laughter spilled from her in a joyous torrent of ecstasy. Harold allowed himself a quick moment to imagine her orgasms. There in the middle of the dining room, on the table linens, maybe even with her husband giving her a standing ovation.

"I still don't believe that they didn't find something wrong with Bill," said Ami. "He was the head of the boy scout chapter."

"Wasn't that pinewood derby thing coming up?" said Harold. "I remember those signs being absolutely everywhere."

"Honey I was in the middle of making a point," said Ami.

"Uh-oh, don't want to be speaking out of turn there," said the shockingly average white man, as he laughed. "Isn't it supposed to be only when spoken to?"

"How could he just walk away from all of that?" continued Ami. "Just leave the block like that. Do you know if they've listed the house with anyone yet?"

"And now the truth comes out," laughed shockingly average white man, as his wife exploded with laughter as she fetched a plate of nachos from the kitchen.

Ami watched in distain as they ate nachos and cackled. She could forgive Harold and the shockingly average white man, but the other woman at the table was making a spectacle of herself. The woman's cackle was like an orgasm, spewing forth across the table and tainting everything it touched. She hadn't been planning on having any nachos anyway, but now watching the shockingly average white man and her husband, suck the grease and orgasm off their fingers, she began to feel ill.

"It's getting late," whined James. "I think it might be close to eleven."

"It's eleven fifteen," said HoJo.

"Eleven fifteen! I told you I needed to be back before eleven fifteen! Why didn't you tell me what time it was?"

"Because, you would leave."

"Of course I would, my parents are home now. Fuck!"

The blue flashing lights of the police cruiser made them both jump. If HoJo hadn't been so distracted, staring at the house, he might have gotten away. His hormonal friend was so obsessed with not getting into trouble; he got away without getting caught. Ironically, it was the hormonal friend's parents who had called the police when they found their son missing.

"Son," said the police officer. "I'm only going to tell you this once; you're straight with me, I'll be straight with you. You lie; I'll fuck you so hard you won't be able to sit for a week. Do you understand me?"

"I snuck out so I could see a girl naked," said HoJo. It pained him to call someone like Kelly McIntyre a mere girl, but he thought it best to speak simply and directly to the officer.

The officer smiled at HoJo. "I think we're going to get on just fine, son. Where do you live?"

Ami lay in bed. The bedroom had been decorated to precision. The bedroom, as well as the house, was a beautiful mix of late Victorian, with just a hint of steam punk to keep it fresh and modern, but not so much as to offend. That was always Ami's motto, "not so much as to offend." Especially in this culture of gluttony and excess, someone had to uphold the bounds of decency and good taste. Ami often fantasized that one-day she would be celebrated for her unwavering discretion and restraint.

Harold came out of the bathroom with "that" look on his face. The one he would put on when he would be inquiring about sex.

"I just checked HoJo's Individuality™ page, and it says he's asleep," said Harold.

There had been a time when Harold's advances had been mildly endearing. It was much better than him actually asking her, the sheer awkwardness of that was almost too much to bear.

For Ami, at this point in their relationship, there was little difference between the actual act of intercourse and masturbation. Both required a minimal amount of effort, and both ended precisely in the same manner, with Harold breathless, and her covered in sweat. Why Harold couldn't deal with these issues himself was a source of constant frustration for Ami.

"I need you to pick up HoJo from school tomorrow," she said, quickly diffusing the situation.

"You know how I hate that," said Harold. "Isn't he old enough to walk home by himself?"

"Harold," she said, taking the lecturing tone, which she knew he hated, but, would ensure that she wouldn't have to endure sex with him this evening. "You know how important it is to appear involved with HoJo. Parental involvement is very important, especially if we want to get a letter of recommendation for high school."

"I know, but I think the boy is old enough to make it home on his own," said Harold. "He can post an update to his Individuality™ page when he gets home."

"Fine," said Ami. "You want to destroy his future, that's fine."

"I don't see how him walking home on his own is destroying his future," said Harold.

The front door bell rang. Harold looked at the alarm clock on his bedside, it clearly read, "11:30".

The door was awash in the strobing blue light of the police cruiser outside. Harold opened it to reveal HoJo and a police officer.

"I think this belongs to you, sir," said the officer trying to sound conversational. "Just to remind you, and your son, curfew for minors is ten thirty."

"Thank you officer," said Harold, as Ami hauled HoJo inside the house. Harold closed the door, as Ami began to quietly berate HoJo. Harold went to the bar and poured himself a drink. He lied to himself saying that it would help him sleep, but as far back as Harold could remember he wasn't a sleeper. He could nap like a pro, but sleeping more than a few hours a night just never came naturally to him.

His therapist had suggested that it had something to do with stress. His doctors could find nothing wrong with him, except for the usual banter they gave about his cholesterol, weight and blood pressure. Harold would nod, and promise to follow whatever guidelines were laid out before him. Once home, however, they would be dismissed. His insomnia never affected his work. He could sleep when tired, but never for very long. There was always something there just on the periphery, something that kept him up.

"Old enough to walk home by himself is he?" hissed Ami from the other room. "You are picking him up tomorrow!"

"Why does he have to pick me up?" protested HoJo. "I hate it when he comes to pick me up!"

Harold finished his drink and closed his eyes and gently began rubbing them. From behind his eyelids light exploded, in a bunch of brilliant blue sparks, which changed to a fiery tunnel.

The lights exploding behind his closed eyes were called pressure phosphenes. By stimulating the eye with gentle pressure, it responds in the only way it knows how, by telling the brain that it is seeing light.

When Harold was a child he loved that it gave him something other to focus on other than his arguing parents. Now it gave him something to focus on other than his wife and son.

Interlude #1
Quiet Desperation

The offices of Individuality™ were bright and airy. They were prominently located in a high rise that was one of the fixtures of the Chicago skyline. Harold, as office manager, had a beautiful corner office. The large social media company was one of the most successful in the world.

Harold fashioned himself as part of the Internet revolution, however he had stumbled into his job simply because, as with most things in Harold's life, he had been in the right place at the right time. Mr. Frankel, the founder of Individuality™, and the alleged inventor of the internet, needed someone to manage the office, so he could spend more time, and money, at his home in Florida. It was rumored that beneath his Florida compound were the servers that stored the actual Internet. Harold had seen the blueprints for Mr. Frankel's compound, but paid little attention to them. Harold had a good grasp of what an amazing resource Individuality™ and the rest of the Internet was, but really didn't, like most people, care how it worked, as long as it did.

Harold had been working for a small insurance company when he walked into a bar where Mr. Frankel had been discussing his difficulties with finding a suitable candidate for the position. After a twenty-minute conversation, Harold had tripled his salary and was giving his two weeks' notice. That was the way with Harold; he just had a lot of dumb luck.

Navigating the quiet, full office, Harold thought back to when he would visit his father's office. The cacophony of typewriters seemed almost abusive. Now, with the recent upgrade from desktop computers to the new tablets, the sounds of the keystrokes were quickly disappearing.

Harold hit the power button on his tablet, and it sprang to life. Calendar announcements and greetings from people he had just passed in the maze of cubicles outside his office, popped up. The focus of this week's communications was the first Individuality™ convention in New Orleans. There were meetings to prepare for meetings to review the presentations and logistics of future meetings. Harold smiled. When he had a secretary, how insurmountable this felt, but now, all the information was here, and with a swipe of a finger he could make changes. In his head he worked backward from the time that he would pick up HoJo. With two more gestures his day was rearranged, and the parties involved were informed of his early departure for the day. There were a few quick protests, which were instant messaged to him, but they were dealt with by referencing the reason why he was leaving early. Say what you will about faceless cold Internet companies, at Individuality™ they understood the importance of family.

As Harold worked his way through the inbox on the tablet, movement outside his office caught his eye. People were standing and walking toward the break kitchen. A loud voice was followed by the sound of glass breaking.

What the hell is going on? Texted Harold.

A quick ping from his tablet told him he had an instant message.

Marc is losing his mind in the break room. Read the instant message.

Harold grabbed his tablet and cautiously followed the crowd.

"I am not going to do it anymore!" screamed Marc. Marc had always been one of the better copywriters. He could quickly come up with new and innovative ways of advertising web spaces. Usually Marc wore a sport coat without a tie, dark pants, and a light shirt. This would be paired with smart looking sneakers in an array of fun colors. Now, however he was standing barefoot in the middle of the break kitchen, his tablet smashed on the tile floor.

I hope he backed everything up. IM'd someone in the crowd. Harold calculated the price of the tablet, as well as made a mental note of which forms he was going to have Marc sign before he was officially terminated.

Has anyone e-mailed security? Texted Harold. He appeared to be the senior man in the room, and thought it best if someone took charge.

"Hello?" said Marc as he stared at the crowd. No one spoke; they glanced down at their tablets, as they pinged. "Let me rephrase that! I said Hello! The proper thing would be to say hello back."

I think Carol was doing that. IM'd one of the interns.

Why don't we make certain that someone did? Texted Harold.

Marc marched out of the white break room and toward the sea of cubicles, the crowed followed.

"Hello!" he screamed shaking the cubicle wall. "Hello!"

My God why doesn't anyone do anything? Pinged one of the new Administrative Assistants.

Marc grabbed a tablet out of the hands of one of the interns. Looking straight into the intern's eyes, Marc screamed, "Hello!"

Harold felt compelled to do something he didn't often do. Marc's behavior was nothing that Harold came close to understanding, but he couldn't stand idly by while Marc decided to become abusive with an intern. The flagrant destruction of company property alone was enough, but abusing an intern was just nasty. So, Harold spoke to his co-worker.

"Hi," said Harold. He felt weightless, terrified.

Marc turned and smiled at him, a broad, insane smile. The tablet slipped from his hand and hit the floor, the screen cracking.

"Hello," said Marc.

"Hi," said Harold.

"See was that so hard?" said Marc to the assembled crowd. "Good morning."

"Hi?" said Harold.

Building security arrived, much to Harold's relief. Marc quietly began to leave with them, but then turned back to Harold, and whispered, "Thank you."

All right everybody back to work. Texted Harold.

Much of the rest of the morning was a wash. Harold tried to keep up with the torrent of texts, IMs and e-mails praising his initiative and bravery. There were even a few suggestions of celebrating after work over a few drinks. Harold's need to pick up HoJo quickly put those plans to rest. Even Mr. Frankel e-mailed him, commending him on his handling of the recent crisis.

Harold wandered through it in a haze. Every communication that came through he saw Marc's insane eyes looking back at him. As he read them, all he could hear was the small and quiet voice, which had said, "Thank you."

Harold closed his eyes and slowly began to rub his eyes. Behind his eyes an explosive tunnel of light swept him away.

Hate

Harold hated picking up HoJo. The long walk up the private path, across the manicured gardens, always reminded him of visiting a cemetery. The tall hedges and gates were to keep the "wrong" people out. This mainly consisted of the white people who couldn't afford to send their children to Ryce Academy and, of course, most brown people.

Ryce always rubbed Harold the wrong way. However, for all intents and purposes, the place was ideal. The test scores were great; the kids got into the best private universities, and went on to prominent positions in politics and business. Ryce Academy had modeled itself on the best British private institutions. When Ami heard that, she envisioned a world of discipline and precision. To sell it to HoJo, she remarked how it was just like Harry Potter. Harold found it to be like the private school Damien attended in the Omen.

Although the grounds were extensive, all of the parents, nannies, and sitters were funneled into a small parking lot, and then led to a small playground area. There they waited in secluded silence for their children.

The different factions had been established long ago, and mingling was fiercely frowned upon. To the east were the Latino nannies. Opposite them, to the west, were the eastern European nannies. In the middle were the "organizing" moms; the ones who made certain that you had your tickets for the next fundraiser, and weren't planning on spending the weekend idle. This left the occasional stragglers who would flit from group to group, grandparents, Men's Service Club members, stay at home dads, and the social outcasts to fend for themselves.

Harold was a proud, longstanding member of the Men's Service Club. The Men's Service Club consisted mainly of finding new and interesting ways to combine drinking, sports, and causes. In March, there would be the March pizza and beer-a-thon to benefit Ryce Academy's science department. In fall there would be the Bear's Fun Run to benefit the Arts programs at Ryce. They would drink heavily and race down the street in a bear suit. In the winter there was both the toy drive as well as the wine festival, to benefit the library and athletic programs respectively. Not to mention the myriad other smaller fundraisers the Men's Club organized.

Unless another member of the Men's Club was there, Harold would stand off to the side, out of the way, trying to look busy with his tablet. This was why, initially, no one noticed he had collapsed.

HoJo hated it when his father came to pick him up. He would either be making loud, rude jokes with some other member of the Men's Club, or looking dejected standing off to the side by himself. At least Mom was good with pretending to interact with the other moms, if for no other reason than to network. She would hand out business cards and smile, never the hard sell. She strove to maintain a distinct level of dignity, and nothing undermined that like a hard sell, it just reeked of desperation.

"Look, you either want the elevator pass or you don't," said HoJo to the kid standing before him in his "office". The third floor boy's restroom had been deserted after Matthew Charles had committed suicide in it three years ago. The kids didn't think that it was haunted, but, out of respect, felt that the right thing to do would be to not use it. HoJo felt that it was the perfect place for a cigarette break, and to update his Individuality™ profile.

HoJo took up smoking; having overheard that Kelly McIntyre had a crush on Jason Fillmore, who smoked. It had taken HoJo a solid year to actually get used to it. Now he could stand to smoke an entire one without puking, but sadly he was now addicted. Usually around third period, and just after lunch, the compulsion to have a cigarette became so all consuming, there were only two choices. Either find a place to sneak a cigarette, or watch his GPA suffer. With Kelly

McIntyre setting her sights on some very selective schools, he was going to have to keep his scores up.

At first, he tried to smoke with the cool kids, but they never used the same place twice. Trying to find where they were each period was exhausting. Then there were the hipster kids, but their affinity for unfiltered cigarettes left HoJo coughing and sputtering. He then tried to smoke with the Goth kids, then the criminals, and then losers. After being ridiculed, mugged, and bored senseless respectively, he found the abandoned restroom. Rarely visited by anyone, including the janitorial staff, he quickly established it as his "office". The relative seclusion also assisted in HoJo's other enterprises. He was going to need money if he was going to sweep Kelly McIntyre off here feet, and maintain his cigarette habit.

"I'm not sure," said the underclassman. "Where did you say the elevator was located?"

"Where did you say it was located?" mocked HoJo, taking a long pull off his cigarette. "Are you tired of getting to class late? Those tardies can pile up."

"You're not supposed to smoke on school grounds," said the underclassman.

"And?" said HoJo, hoping to sound less like he just got caught, and more like he didn't care.

"My Nana died, because she smoked," said the underclassman. HoJo tried to think of something to say as quickly as he could. Although conceptually he knew that cigarette smoking could lead to lung cancer this was the first time that anyone had said that it might kill specifically him.

The door to the restroom shot open. HoJo instinctively tossed the cigarette out the window. Peering up innocently at whoever had burst into his office. The hormonal one he had spent the previous night's exploits with stood there trying to catch his breath.

"Ah, if it isn't the world's worst look out," said Harold, pulling out a fresh cigarette and lighting it. "You know I caught hell last night. I know what you're going to say. If we'd had left when you wanted us to, I wouldn't have gotten into trouble. But dude what happened? You just left me there. Not cool, dude, not cool at all."

"Dude," said James. "I think your dad's dead."

Ami hated showing the Dordek house. It was a big, drafty Victorian that had been redone in the fifties. When it was redone, they removed any of the charm a Victorian might offer and instead filled it with the worst of fifties kitsch: The ugly linoleum in the dated kitchen. The pale green tiles in the master bath, paired with a modern chrome and glass shower, standing next to a stained glass window. The bedrooms were small, but the closets huge. Even the original oak floors sported a thick orange and brown shag carpet.

"The property itself has only had three owners, which in its hundred and thirty years of existence is pretty rare," she said to the couple. She knew they wouldn't like it, and on the remote chance they did, she knew that they couldn't afford it. This was the asinine part, if the child who had inherited the property were to cut the price to something reasonable; she might be able to move it. If the kid were willing to sink some money into making the damned place livable, she might be able to get the exorbitant asking price. But, this schmuck was not going to budge.

"Did you notice the fireplace in the kitchen," said Ami. "That'll cut down on those pesky heating bills come winter."

"Was that what was next to the rock wall?" said the male part of the couple. "I wasn't quite certain what the hell that was."

"Well now you know it was a fireplace," said Ami. "Did you notice the view of the lake?"

"No," said the female part of the couple.

"It is of course much easier to see in the winter," said Ami. "See the white Georgian across the street?"

The couple peered over toward the house. It was a gorgeous home. Ami silently thought a quick affirmation before continuing. I will sell this house. I will sell this house. I will sell this mother-fucking piece of shit of a house. These morons will buy this house. But, she knew they wouldn't. Her cell phone rang. Damnit. Damnit. Damnit. She thought. Looking down she saw it was a call from the Ryce Academy.

"Will you both excuse me for a moment?" pleaded Ami, trying to sound sincere but not subservient, just like the tapes had taught her. "It's my son's school." The couple gave her a quick nod and went off to giggle and mock a house they couldn't afford.

If that fat bastard forgot to pick up his own goddamned son, she thought. The she took a deep breath, sounding as composed as she could she placed the cell to her ear and said, "Hello?"

HoJo emerged from the third floor boys' room, to find a crowd of people pressed into the hallway. It was clear they had been discussing who would be the one to go in and inform him about his father. It had been lucky for them that James, the hormone, had been walking by when he did. The crowd parted before him. As he walked they fell in behind him, and followed. This was the way the Ryce Academy operated. It was the duty of your peers to fall in behind and help you in our time of need. It was largely a symbolic gesture, and most days it made HoJo want to vomit. But, today was different. First, it was him whom they were all standing behind. Second, and most importantly, Kelly McIntyre was walking directly behind him. He hadn't been able to see her naked last night, but if he played is cards right, he might just get the opportunity out of sheer sympathy.

How to play it was HoJo's big question? Should he, on seeing his dead father, show how sensitive he could be by falling to pieces, or would he come across as a blubbering fool? Or, thought HoJo, should I play the anger? That all of this might be some kind of horrible mistake, this death not only wrongs me, but also him. Maybe, thought HoJo, if I'm really lucky he was violently murdered, and I can play the Bruce Wayne vigilante angle. I need your help Kelly to find my father's killer. Or, he could play the bad ass. If she didn't like it, he could just blame it on the fact that he was in shock. Hell, if his father really was dead, there was going to be a hell of a lot that he was going to be able to get away with. It is substantially brilliant! Please be dead, pleaded HoJo in his head.

HoJo walked out the main door, which lead to the playground. His father lay prone on the black top. One of the gym teachers was busy attempting CPR. HoJo pulled a cigarette from his pocket, and lit it. Most of the kids gasped at his audacity, which was just the reaction he had been hoping for. He took a long drag off the cigarette and looked deeply into Kelly McIntyre's eyes. He tried to conjure up the idea of someone brooding and intense, possibly even smoldering. Luckily for him, most of the kids were so focused on the cigarette that they didn't notice that he looked constipated.

Then he turned, and walked back inside.

Ami was allowing herself to fantasize. She tried to temper the thought that Harold might be dead, with the lie that the couple might have actually put in an offer on the Dordeck house. She knew they wouldn't, but it was difficult to keep down he swell of joy she felt. She might actually be free of Harold! No longer would she have to concern herself with having to fend off his advances. No longer would she have to make excuses for his crass behavior, or deal with his Men's Service Club assholes. No longer would she have to pick up after the lazy bastard, she thought. Because, the fat bastard is dead! She couldn't suppress the cackle any longer. It began as a harmless giggle then grew uncontrollably into a full torrent of laughter, which continued to grow more violently orgasmic.

Ami fought to regain control, but the more she fought the louder she became. Forty years of suppressed laughter exploded from her, rattling the doors on the minivan. She laughed so hard, she wet herself. This, she would later blame on the accident. There was no way she could have seen neither the red light, nor the police cruiser as the minivan swerved and slammed into the back of it.

Initially, Harold was frightened. His orientation quickly went from vertical to horizontal. That can be highly disconcerting. Then, however, he began to let go. He was surprised at how easily things began to fall away from him. The first things he began to forget about were his sports teams, which he followed avidly. Once that concern was gone he felt a bit lighter. Then he lost the need to keep the lawn and the house looking good, which caused him to feel lighter. He felt as if he were hovering just slightly above the surface of the asphalt. Then the need to impress his friends fell away and he floated higher. Then the need to impress the people he didn't know fell away, and he floated higher. The need to excel in his profession fell away, and he floated higher.

As Harold brought his thoughts back toward his family, he realized that he was floating higher than the school. He was looking down on the grounds. He thought about HoJo, and how much better he would be with someone who was a more appropriate role model. That was how Ami put it. He thought about Ami, and how much their routine had been pretty miserable lately. None of them had been enjoying his life, especially not him, and he let it all go.

As he was about to untether himself, the part of his brain, the part which was cut off from its blood supply, died; remarkably, to compensate, Harold's brain woke up another area. An area that had been dormant for a very long time, a part that held the truth about Harold, and his existence; for the first since his stroke began, Harold wanted to live. He knew the truth, and the truth of so many others; others who continually made themselves miserable, blindly following a pre-programmed need to belong.

Finally, Harold knew why none of it meant anything. Why he needed to be seen as someone who was important. Why he worried about his lawn. Why he wanted to watch millionaires with his friends. He, and so many people like him had been making themselves miserable, because they had been programmed to assimilate; programmed to need to belong. Harold was part of an invasion. Harold was an alien.

Truth

Harold opened his eyes and stared at the grey ceiling. He liked the way that it matched the green-grey walls of the room. He smiled briefly at the color plate, giving it a quick nod of approval, and then looked and smiled at Terrance. Harold knew his name was Terrance because it was on his visitor's tag, which was haphazardly stuck to his left shoulder, upside down. He was a beautiful man. Something that Harold would have hesitated to acknowledge before he knew the truth. Terrence was clearly of Middle Eastern decent. He stared back at Harold with his dark eyes, he didn't look as if he had been caught, but he didn't look as relaxed as he had a minute ago.

"Is this a hospital?" said Harold. Terrence stared at him. "I think I had a stroke, or a heart attack, or something like that."

"Stroke?" said Terrence.

"Thank heavens," said Harold.

"I don't think I've ever met someone who was happy to have a stroke before," said Terrence.

"It makes more sense if it was a stroke, said Harold. "You're the first person, of your kind I've ever met, and not been afraid of."

"And exactly what kind of person is that," said Terrence, in the same flat Midwestern accent as Harold.

"Umm, you know the first person that's from where you're from," said Harold. "After everything happened with those airplanes, and those buildings."

"Don't remember any of them being from Detroit," said Terrence. "What you see someone with dark skin, dark eyes, and dark hair, you just assume that I'm some kind of terrorist."

"See, if this was before I knew what I now know," said Harold. "I'd be scared of people from the Middle East. But, now I know I really don't need to be frightened by you, or people like you."

"But, fat, white, bigoted, crazy Midwesterners, are terrifying," said Terrence.

"You can say that again," said Harold. "Oh, I see where you might be mistaken, but I am not from the Midwest."

"Sorry, I just see pudgy milk fed white people and I just assume," said Terrence. "So, you're an east coast bigot. You're much to pale to be from the west coast, again making assumptions. I don't hear a drawl, so I don't think you're from the south. Wait, are you Canadian?"

"I'm from a bit farther away than that," said Harold. "Do you mind if I ask you a question, Terrence?"

"If I say yes, will you ask it anyway?"

"Probably."

"Then, go ahead."

"Have you ever had an uncontrollable urge to join larger and more popular groups?"

"What? Like a mosque?"

"Sure, it could be a mosque. How about this? Are you a sports fan?"

"Not really. I'll watch the occasional game, but I wouldn't say that I was an avid fan."

"Oh," said Harold, sounding disappointed.

"You are Canadian! Do you want to talk hockey? I am from Detroit, but I had a life."

"No, not at all," said Harold. "You see if you were like me, then I would be able to set you free from all of that nagging need to belong. But, I think you're actually human."

"And you aren't?"

"Me?" said Harold. "Goodness, no. I'm an energy signature from just to the left of galactic center. We, the rest of my invasion force, came in search of a new home."

"Wow," said Terrence. "Because, you look just like a fat, white bigot. Not an energy signature at all. You are crazy aren't you?"

"I know how it must seem," said Harold. "But, this is how one of my kind acts when no longer bound by the programming."

"That clears it all up, thank you."

"I'm very happy I could help. What are you doing in my room?"

"Well, I was planning on stealing the cash out of your wallet, but it doesn't seem right- Since you're crazy and all."

"I'm sorry; I don't have any cash on me. Or at least I didn't before I woke up here. But, I did have an ATM card. Do you need some money?"

"Not exactly need," said Terrence. "I just have a strange compulsion to steal money out of the wallets of white people and give it to the homeless."

"So they can get something to eat? That's really very noble of you."

"Actually, I give it to them so that they can get themselves something to drink. It helps with the random causality of the universe."

"I'll let you use my ATM card, but you have to let me come with you."

"That's sweet of you, but I have a standing rule against taking money from crazy people."

"Please, you can't leave me here. My wife will be coming."

"What do you have against your wife?" said Terrence. "Did she try to kill you?"

"No, but she will try to stop me. Make me back into the way that I was."

"I don't think that would be the best of ideas."

"Please."

"Look I'm certain that you are a very nice alien, but there is no way I'm going to take you out of this hotel."

"Why not?"

"Fuck you. Why?"

"Because of one very blatant reason. Anyone could see it in your eyes or smell it on you. It's in everything from the way you walk, the way you dress, the choices of words. Terrence, you are desperately bored, and have been for some time. You are searching for anything to lift you out of this quagmire of mundane. I can help with that."

"Let me get a wheelchair."

Ami had given herself a moment to adjust to the idea of being a widow. It excited her. She had the kind of figure where black really was slimming, not the kind of figure where people lie to you, and tell you that black is slimming. The thought of being able to get rid of all of Harold's crap, made her giggly again. Now that she wouldn't have to compete with Harold for HoJo, things could finally get accomplished, the way only she knew they needed to, around the house.

The first thing to go would be Harold Junior's stupid nickname. Then the eating habits would be examined. HoJo was not going to have to endure what she had to endure in High school. He would be fit, and popular, and Harold wouldn't be there to interfere, with his gut and nachos. She would, of course, have to take it slow. Harold had only had only died a few hours ago. Harold Junior had just lost his father, it would take time to erase the memory and create the new one she planed. She could create a martyr out of her dead husband, and mold it to her advantage. That was the way you made mother fucking lemonade out of lemons, she thought. She allowed herself another giggle. In the parking lot of the hospital, she adjusted her makeup, and put on a fittingly sallow look.

The lobby of the hospital had been recently re-done, in what had been described to the board, a healing palette of color. Ami thought it looked beige. The receptionist was young, thin, and happy. The receptionist liked beige. If Ami knew this, it would cause her to dislike her even more.

"Hi, how can I direct you?" asked the receptionist.

"Yes my husband was brought in," said Ami. "I'm here, I believe, to identify his body." Ami fought the feelings of joy she felt deep inside. Giggling now might seem insensitive.

"Oh, I am so sorry for you loss," said the girl. She sounded sincere, which bothered Ami even more. "What was his name?"

"Harold Winestock," said Ami.

"Your relationship to the deceased?" said the Receptionist, as she typed the name into the computer. "I don't mean to sound like an idiot, but they ask me to ask these things."

"It's quite alright," lied Ami. "As I said, I am, or rather, I was his wife."

"Oh, you poor thing," said the receptionist. "Had you been married long?"

Ami, instead of continuing to answer the receptionist's insipid questions, simply nodded in agreement as she pulled a tissue from her bag.

"Oh, it's alright," said the receptionist. "You just let it all out. Feel free to become a blubbering mess right here. There is nothing to be embarrassed about. Did you have any kids?"

Ami nodded, as she dabbed her eyes and extended her middle finger.

"Just the one, well I'm certain he, or she, will be your rock through this, your time of need," said the Receptionist. "Is the child with you at the moment?"

Ami shook her head.

"Well that's good, because minors aren't allowed in the morgue," said the receptionist. "Let me just see where to send you. The computers are working very slowly today. They're in the middle of a server upgrade."

"If you could just tell me where the morgue is," said Ami. "I'll head down there myself."

"Now, I know that you're entering your anger phase," said the receptionist. "And I respect that, but it won't make the computers work any faster."

A line was quickly growing behind Ami.

"I'm sorry you're right," said Ami. "There is no reason I should take my grief-"

"Oh, my God!" screamed the receptionist. "This is like a miracle. Either that or it's a glitch in the computer system. I don't want to get your hopes up, but I would really rather think that it's a miracle."

"What?"

"Harold's not dead!"

"Fuck you," said Ami.

"I'm sorry," said the receptionist. "This really is horrible to do to you, especially if it ends up being an accident. But, if it isn't, just think about it."

"Fuck you," said Ami, she pulled out another tissue and began to cry. This was just like Harold. To take something a beautiful, the moment of his own death, and shit all over it. What a fucking asshole, thought Ami. Ami looked around at the line of people staring at her. Ami quickly concluded that she had actually said it out loud, not just thought it.

"It's okay," said the receptionist. "You were in your anger phase, and sometimes, if that's derailed it can manifest itself in some of the strangest ways. I think you might even be going into shock."

"That was pretty intense," said Kelly McIntyre.

"Yeah, I know," said HoJo, trying his best not to let his voice crack. His palms were visibly dripping with sweat. Attempting to smoke was useless, because the paper would be soaked through. This was everything he had dreamed about. He was with Kelly McIntyre in her bedroom. And she had kissed him! Kelly smiled at him, and he nearly wet himself.

"So where is your Mom?" asked Kelly.

"She went to identify the body," said HoJo.

"Wow," said Kelly. "I don't know how you're dealing with this so well. You're pretty hard core."

"I know," said HoJo. "So can I see your underwear?"

"Sure," said Kelly

HoJo blacked out.

Of all the dumb ass things to have happened to her, thought Ami. First, she gets stuck with the chipper thin young thing at the reception desk. Then she's told that the fat bastard might have lived. It sounded like something he would do. The receptionist even gave her the wrong room number. Waiting in the long line the receptionist caught her eye and smiled and waved. The little thing even had the audacity to give her an inquisitive thumb up. Ami had never been one for empty gestures, the "thumbs up" being one of her least favorite. The line marched slowly toward the receptionist, who was chipper and lovely with everyone. Ami really did consider doing horrible things to her, and it brought a smile to her face, which was misinterpreted by the receptionist.

"It is awfully good to see you again, too," said the receptionist. "How may I help?"

"I think you may have given me the wrong room number," said Ami, still smiling.

"Well with the work they've been doing on the servers it wouldn't surprise me," said the receptionist. "Your husband's name was?"

"Harold Winestock," said Ami, fighting a sneer.

"That's right," said the receptionist, as she typed the name into the computer. "Oops! Looks like you two missed each other. Right after you left me to head up to the room, his friend showed up to discharge him."

"You're telling me that you discharged my husband," said Ami. "My husband, who has gone from dead, to not dead, to not here? Didn't you want to keep him for observation to see what the hell caused him to possibly be dead in the first place?!"

"Now, Mrs. Winestock, I know you must be going through an entire series of emotions right now," said the receptionist. "But, this had to be some kind of a glitch with the server update. I really think that-"

"Stop talking!" said Ami. "Just stop fucking talking; I need you to find me someone in charge here. Someone, whom I may scream at, and threaten with legal action; I need to know where my husband is right now."

HoJo couldn't believe his luck. He was moments away from seeing, what he had been waiting most of his life to see: Kelly McIntyre in her underwear. The room was as he had imagined it. Light pastel wallpaper, a bookshelf full of novels, which he made a note to read soon. The unicorn obsession, however, had been a bit of a surprise. He sat on the white iron day bed, and thought briefly about laying down, but feared that it might look a little strange, maybe even a little "gay". The one thing that no thirteen-year-old boy could possibly be caught being; it was the clear kiss of death.

HoJo heard the phone ringing in the other room. "Hold that thought," said Kelly, rising to answer the phone. "I'll be right back."

If he were lucky maybe it would be his mother, distraught after seeing the body of his dead father. Then he could move to phase two of his plan. He would show his sensitive, but not homo, side to Kelly McIntyre, insuring that he would be able to actually touch her underwear. His father had never been this much help to him while he had been alive, but now in death he was the man! He could kiss the magnificent, dead bastard.

Kelly opened the door with a broad smile on her face. Dare he dream, thought HoJo, could it be possible that she was just as excited to show him her underwear, as he was to see it?

"HoJo," she said, so happy she was almost crying. "Your dad is alive."

"Fuck," said HoJo.

Harold was enjoying quite a few firsts. This was the first time he had ever ridden in a wheelchair, and to be honest, he was enjoying it. This was the first time he had a friend of Arab decent; which made him both happy and sad. He was happy to have a new friend, but regretted the years spent fearing people like Terrence. This was the first time he had left his wife. Harold hesitated painting her like some monster. She could be a lot of fun. Ami was just obsessed with doing things the "right" way. Harold briefly entertained the thought that she might also be an alien, but quickly dismissed it. He had too much to accomplish. The world was vivid and vibrant. The smells were amazing. The sky was bluer than he remembered. Very different then the fiery sky above his home planet. He felt like someone who had finally purchased a color television set. The birds chirped on cue.

"Are you sure you want to do this, man?" asked Terrence.

"No," said Harold. "And I doubt I'll really ever be sure of anything ever again. But, it feels good. Do you know what I mean?"

"No, I don't," said Terrence. "But, I'm not going to look this gift horse in the mouth."

"So, what do they usually drink," said Harold.

"I don't usually hang around to find out," said Terrence.

"So, you're kind of like a Robin Hood," said Harold. "Why do you work in a hospital? Is it so you can get close to the money? I would think that that might become a liability towards you getting hired. If people keep getting robbed where ever you go."

"I don't work at the hospital," said Terrence. "I have to serve out my community service hours."

"Community service?"

"I'm a terrorist."

Interlude #2

Addiction

Terrence enjoyed growing up in Detroit. He liked school, had quite a few friends and, he reaped the benefits of a poorly planned suicide. His high school had been looking for a new drama teacher for months. There were a few candidates that seemed suitable, but none with the kind of resume that people of the small Detroit suburb demanded for their children.

There was little doubt that Zach White was qualified. He had been in the chorus for every major Broadway hit for the past twenty years. The paychecks were meager, but steady. He had watched everyone from Bob Fosse to Joel Grey Direct. Obsessed with watching their work, he knew that one day he would have the opportunity to move from the chorus to a supporting role. When Zack had his chance, he wanted to be one step ahead of every director. Then, they would comment on what a joy he was to work with. How he was such an intuitive actor, always knowing precisely what was needed to set a scene on fire. Then by virtue of his reputation alone he would become a star.

Unfortunately, as was the case with 99.99% of people with whom he worked with in the chorus, he never got his break. He slowly aged out of the chorus and the roles he hoped to immortalize.

There was very little else to be done. On a whim, while watching his savings slowly dwindle he responded to a small ad in the back of one of the trades for a teaching position in a small suburb of Detroit.

"Have you ever even been to Detroit?" said Ovid, the bartender.

"Yes, when we did the revival tour of Carousel," said Zach, as he drained another martini.

"Try to make them last," said Ovid. "There are only so many that I can float you before people begin to take notice."

"I'm sick of it," said Zack. "Why the hell am I going to bust my ass to stay here? I'm beginning to loathe Manhattan."

"That's because you can't afford to do anything," said Ovid, as he poured Zack another. "The only people who hate Manhattan are the ones who can't afford it."

"Don't be like that."

"You know it's true, half of Florida is populated by actors who couldn't afford it anymore. That's why they have so much goddamned dinner theatre down there."

"At least in Detroit I could make a living, save a bit of money, and have some extra at the end of the week."

"Yes darling, but there isn't anything to spend it on. What are you going to do on your hot Friday night? Catch a Red Wings game?"

"What the hell am I supposed to do?"

"How the fuck should I know? I'm just a bartender with a soft spot for chorus boys. But, as my father always said; Those who can do, do. Those who can't, teach."

Those words followed Zach home, cutting him deeply.

He hadn't thought about stopping at the hardware store. But, under the harsh fluorescent lighting, he lingered by the drain cleaner, and thought it might be too painful. He saw he razor blades, and thought of the mess. He saw the extension cords, and envisioned the drama of friends finding him swinging from the lone light fixture in his studio.

He walked up the six flights of stairs, looking at his mail. There it was, a large envelope with a Detroit postmark.

He walked into the five hundred square foot apartment. He had taken great care to decorate it. His use of space had gotten masterful over the years.

He pulled out the thirty-foot extension cord. He had worked on enough shows, that he was competent to tie a solid knot. Within minutes he had made a noose, which he slipped through the lighting fixture. He thought about leaving a note, but any mystery surrounding his death would only add to the drama.

Zack climbed on the back of one of the dining room chairs, placed the noose around his neck, and jumped.

Zack misjudged the length of the noose and the strength of the lighting fixture. He landed hard on the floor, and the lighting fixture landed on his head. Ovid's words echoed in his head, "Those that can do, do; those who can't, teach."

Unable to even kill himself, he put the breakdown behind him and found himself teaching drama at a small school in suburban Detroit.

Zack had been conducting auditions at Anderson Douglas High School for the past three days. Determined that his production was going to be not only one of the best productions of Fiddler on the Roof that the small Detroit suburb had ever seen, but his innovative stage design, placing the chorus actually in the orchestra pit, bringing them out in front of the action on stage, would make his premiere production one of legend. Sadly, he still had not found his Tevye.

"Why are you stressing about it, it's just kids," said Ovid; since the move to the Midwest Zack found himself calling Ovid more often. He lied to himself, pretending the reason he called was to keep up with what was happening in New York. The truth lay somewhere between his need to validate his choices and nostalgia.

"You don't understand," said Zack. "This isn't some kind of prep for state thespians; we're talking about the spring musical."

"That's what you've been saying for the past two months. But, if you don't make this fun for the kids then they'll never learn anything. This isn't about your ego; this is about the kids, right?"

What a moron, thought Zack. Of course this was about his ego. What the hell had he been doing by watching all of those other directors if not to arrive at this very moment? Delusion can be a powerful thing.

"I know that, but I just want to find the best Tevye that I can."

"Why the hell did you decide to do Fiddler at a school full of Arabs?"

"Don't you limit them, don't you dare limit my kids. Did anyone ever tell you that you couldn't do something because you were gay?"

"I couldn't join the army, but then I never really wanted to. I always saw the military as one long gym class, full of all the jocks that wanted to beat the shit out of you, with guns, killing, and travel. Never sounded like much fun."

"Don't make this about you, please," said Zack. "I might just scream if you make this all about you."

"Why, so we can make it all about you?"

"No, about the kids."

"I need to go," said Ovid.

"Can I call you tomorrow?"

"Do I have a choice?"

The next morning, Zack was summoned to the Vice Principals office. The Vice Principal was a vindictive and manipulative man who was convinced that the spring musical was a waste time and resources.

Sitting outside the Vice-principal's office was Terrence. Terrence was there for some foolish infraction of some silly regulation. Zack watched the way he moved, listened to the way he spoke, and the way he listened to others. Zack had found his Tevye. Zack didn't listen to a word that the vice principal said. He blindly agreed.

"The boy sitting outside of your office, what did he do?"

"Terrence?" said he Vice Principal. "Usual repeat offender who has mild issues with authority; He's probably here because he did something stupid to get out of class because he was bored. It's shits like him that clog up my office. Don't you think I could be doing better things than dealing with a little shit like that?"

"I'm certain that you do."

"I really should make an example of him, probably suspend him."

"I think I might have a better idea."

Terrence's parents, as they often reminded him, had immigrated to the states in the vain hope that they could provide a better life for their children. The idea of actually raising Terrence in Beirut was out of the question. So they settled for an affluent, mainly Lebanese-American, Detroit suburb. Terrence, at times, wanted to make his parents proud. But, the harsh reality was that Terrence was bored. So completely and totally mind numbingly bored with the entire High School experience that he needed to find ways to entertain himself. Unfortunately, the ways in which he found to entertain himself were often frowned upon by the student code of conduct. This was how he had such an intimate understanding of the workings in the vice principals office. Few of the administrators saw him as much of a threat to the stability of the school. They were more concerned with the larger issues of weapons, drugs, and educating the kids. Terrence was rarely a distraction, and the way he got into trouble was so wonderfully creative, that no one really minded. That is, of course, excluding the Vice Principal. The Vice Principal saw the anti social behavior, which Terrence exhibited, as not only detrimental to the school, but clearly undermined what little authority he imagined he had. The thought of actually embarrassing the little shit by having him take a part in some crappy production was just too good to be true.

Terrence approached it as he did most things, with a slight air of bored trepidation. This, however, did not last very long. Zack was so pleased to finally have found his Tevye, that he threw himself into the production with such enthusiasm, such feelings of joy, and such an infectious love of the theater, that there was no way anyone involved this inaugural production wasn't imbued with the same passion for musical theatre.

Zack challenged Terrence on his acting choices, vocal technique, and physicality. There was so much that Terrence was constantly learning between lines, songs, and technique, which he found himself completely engaged.

The production of Fiddler was a masterpiece. Zack followed it up with Arsenic and Old Lace, which then led to Sweeney Todd. Terrence played the lead in all three productions. He loved the challenges that each new character brought. He also loved how quickly it all changed from one production to another. Zack was pleased to see what a great actor Terrence was blossoming into. The work culminated into Terrence's senior year, which Zack staged the full six hour Angels in America saga, to rave reviews.

"You know you have to give it a try," said Zack. "You'll be doing the world a disservice if you don't share your talent with the rest of the world. There are those who will tell you that you shouldn't. That you should go to some conservatory and get more training, but you have so much natural talent, that if you don't attempt to give it a try, it will be a great tragedy."

"I don't know Mr. White; my parents are pretty hell bent on my going to college."

This was an understatement. Terrence's parents had been saving for his college education since he was six months old. At that time a Newsweek article had declared that the average family was going to have to save over three million dollars just to afford college for their children. Regardless of this figure being grossly overblown, it still meant that every extra paycheck they received went toward Terrence's education. This was why his father worked three jobs, his mother two. The only reason she didn't work three jobs was simply because they wanted to insure that there was someone there when Terrence got home.

"But, Mr. White says that I need to grab this opportunity when I can," said Terrence as he tried to explain it to his stone faced parents.

"I am certain that he says a lot of things," said his father. "But, I don't understand why this opportunity won't be there after you get your degree."

The thought of having to face another four years of mind numbing boredom as he waded through a curriculum designed around classes that he just couldn't give a fuck about, seemed too much to bare. That was why he ran away from home to live with his cousin, Andy, in Los Angeles.

For Terrence Los Angeles was a shocking disappointment. He thought was entering a town full of artists waiting to create. Instead, when he pulled up to his cousin Andy's apartment on the corner of Sixth and Kenmore in Koreatown, he found a Los Angeles filled with desperate people vying for a paycheck, begging for work. A society built upon the backs of other minorities hoping for a better life. The entertainment industry was desperate to market, and frightened to create. In short, it had quite a bit in common with Detroit.

Terrence had arrived in Los Angeles on September 11th, 2001. Walking along the street trying to explore Koreatown on September 14th, he was spit on, yelled at, had a can of soda thrown at his head, and signed an agent. He tried to explain to the Agent, as he had to many other people, that he wasn't a terrorist, but just a kid from Detroit. No one, especially the Agent, cared. Terrence quickly began his professional acting career, which consisted of a steady diet of terrorist roles in both film and television.

The roles were not challenging, but they paid well. He and the other Arab American actors he met, none of whom could actually speak Arabic, worked out their own pigeon Arabic to please the Directors and Producers. Soon, they had become so good at the pretend Arabic that they taught it to newer actors.

This steady stream of roles made Terrence very comfortable. He soon moved from the small one bedroom apartment in Korea town, to a small one-bedroom apartment in Santa Monica.

However, Terrence, having grown up in Detroit was not accustomed to the way that time passes in a place like Southern California. Terrence had grown up with the changing of the seasons to mark the passage of time. In Southern California there are no seasons. Eight years passed in the blink of an eye.

Terrence's first nervous breakdown began on April 11th, 2009. He was between jobs at the time, so his reputation was intact. But, for three days he could speak nothing, but his invented Arabic, and the word fuck. This caused a bizarre spiral as he wandered the streets muttering to himself and occasionally screaming an expletive. His cousin Andy found him passed out on a sofa in an alleyway behind his building.

Andy slowly nursed him back to health, but afterwards he would never be the same. For Terrence, acting just wasn't fun anymore. This wasn't the world he had found on stage with Mr. White, a different role, and a different challenge every few months. In fact, the repetition of playing the same cartoonish stereotype had become completely abhorrent to him.

"You need to get the hell out of this city," said his cousin, Andy. "You've been at it for too long, you need to relax. Go to Europe, have some fun."

"You know I've heard of this tea shop in Japan," said Terrence. "It is at the top of a mountain. The only way to get to the teashop is to climb the mountain. At the top they sell two kinds of tea. The first is basically the equivalent of fifty cents. The second is ten thousand dollars."

"You want to climb a mountain in Japan and be over charged," said Andy.

"No, I'm not saying that," said Terrence. "All I'm saying is that I'm looking for something a bit more interesting, than just flying to Europe and drinking."

"Do you know where the tea shop is?"

"Not exactly."

"Do you have ten grand to blow on a cup of tea?"

"No."

"Let's get drunk and go to Paris."

Terrence remembered ordering another round of drinks, finding his passport, and going to the airport with his cousin. The rest was a blur lights, turbulence, and being violently sick in the airplane bathroom. Arriving at the Charles De Gaulle Airport, there was something remotely resembling a cab ride, and then a bed.

Terrence slept off the hangover, the jet lag, and woke late the next afternoon. He felt like someone had taken a shit in his mouth. There was no sign of Andy. The other bed appeared to not have been slept in. After figuring out how to use the shower, and inadvertently the bidet, he went exploring.

Terrence didn't understand Paris. He didn't speak French. He didn't plan the trip, nor research Paris. Terrence found himself awash in the sea of a strange culture, bobbing along with the flotsam and jetsam of every day Parisian life.

After the second day of his cousin missing, Terrence was concerned, but not worried. By the fifth day of not knowing what had happened, Terrence fell into a panic.

The small police station looked like something out of a cheap detective novel. The green paint on the walls was beginning to peel revealing the crumbling red brick underneath.

"My cousin," said Terrence, slowly and loudly to the two uniformed men behind the desk. "I haven't seen him in three days, almost four nights!"

The men behind the counter looked at him quizzically. The one on the right moved as if to say something, but then thought better of it.

"MY COUSIN," he tried again, at a different decibel. "Does anyone here speak English?"

The other uniform whispered, "American."

"Yes, I am American," said Terrence. "Can you help me?"

The two men in uniform spoke to each other for a moment, then the first wrote an address on a piece of paper.

"What is this?"

"American Embassy."

"So are you telling me that you won't help me? Or that you can't help me? Both?"

The two men in uniform began talking to each other. The only word that Terrence could make out was, American. The walk back to the hotel was eerily quiet. Alone with his thoughts he began to fantasize about trying to find his cousin by himself. If the police weren't going to be of any help, why shouldn't he look into it? This could become the grand adventure he had been looking for, like something out of a Robert Ludlum novel. He could make a few inquiries before going the Embassy to be stared at, patted down, and have his story ridiculed. Then he could single-handed discover some huge plot that needed to be stopped. Terrence knew his fantasy sounded vague, but hoped that as events unfolded he would quickly be able to fill in the details.

Up the block from the hotel was a small Absinthe bar; this was here where it began. Terrence spent the first fifteen minutes in the bar frantically asking about his cousin. The two men behind the bar quickly became annoyed with the American who was bothering their loyal customers and the stoned tourists. Pretending not to understand a word that Terrence was saying, the bartender placed a small glass of absinthe in front of Terrence, and insisted that he drink it. Terrence, being American, saw the green mouthwash looking substance as a challenge.

As he tipped the glass back and swallowed, the world tilted slightly to the left. This was what had been missing. The world exploded in a fantastic mix of swirling colors and magnificent tactile emotions. Terrence quickly ordered a second, then a third, then a fourth. He was amazed at the different ways it was served to him. First as a simple shot, then served over a flaming lump of sugar, then with another liquor floated on top, it was actually set aflame. Terrence smiled and walked out into the oppressive and confusing city, and it began to make sense to him. He could see precisely who the tourists were, who the lovers were. Who was wandering the streets hopelessly, and who was desperately clinging to some out dated ideal of the way the world should be. He walked along the river whistling. He had found a way to feel at one with the confusing city around him, a way to let go of the worries of everyday.

As with most addicts, Terrence thought the new substance he had found to be the panacea to all, of not just his, but many of his friend's problems. He spent the next month in a green haze. Sampling a world of Absinthe across Paris, and hatched a plan to bring Absinthe, and its liberation, to the states.

The three cases of absinthe were surprisingly easy to obtain. The four cases of mouthwash however were a bit problematic. Terrence was meticulous in emptying the bottles of mouthwash and refilling them with the absinthe. Terrence often giggled at the simple brilliance of his plan. There were piles of paperwork to be processed, which Terrence, now viewing himself as the new liberator of the western world, promptly ignored. Instead he bribed the few people he met at the airport, assuring them that the bottles of green mouthwash did not contain explosives, but instead contained a legal (in France) mind altering substance. Unfortunately, none of the people he actually bribed were responsible for him getting the "mouthwash" through customs. Most smiled, and wondered why this American was planning on going through all the trouble of smuggling something he could easily pick up at the duty free shop.

He contacted his cousin, who had made his way back to Los Angeles. There were questions about where and how they had been separated, but eventually Andy reluctantly agreed to pick him up at the airport. He said it in a flippant way, which annoyed Terrence. Andy didn't understand that he was on a mission of liberation. This wasn't his addiction talking.

Very little went according to plan. In the days he spent planning; Terrence had kept meaning to get an alarm clock. The digital clock in the hotel room was unreliable at best, but more often than not, downright deceptive. There was a long list of things that needed addressing before Terrence could leave. All of these were ignored in favor of consumption of more Absinthe.

Due to the lack of a working alarm clock, Terrence found himself tearing through Charles De Gaulle Airport, screaming for the gate attendant to hold the plane for him. If he had taken care of the paperwork, Terrence's three cases of mouthwash might have ended up on the correct plane. Terrence in his rush also boarded the wrong plane. Fortunately, it was the same wrong plane that contained his cases of Absinthe. Unfortunately, this plane would get grounded in Chicago due to a blizzard.

On the ground in Chicago, the TSA agents grilled him. They wanted to know why some Arab kid was so interested in mouthwash. When the liquid inside the bottles of was tested for explosives, it came back negative. However, Terrence's questioning by the TSA landed him on a no-fly list.

"How the hell am I supposed to get home?" said Terrence.

"Maybe you should have considered that before you boarded the wrong flight with a bunch of mouthwash," said the uniformed woman.

He might not have made it home, but he still had the three cases of liberation. Terrence made another call to

Andy, who moaned at the thought of a road trip to the Midwest.

A quick cab ride with his precious gifts found him in a cheap hotel in a Chicago suburb, across the street from a mall. Terrence saw it as a bastion of hell, but hopefully his wait wouldn't be long.

"Is there anywhere to eat?" Terrence asked the man at the front desk, his nametag claimed his name was Mike. Terrence had always been suspicious of people with nametags. The opportunity for flagrant fraud was just too much. How the hell was he to know that the man with the nametag was actually who he said he was?

"There are quite a few places both in the food court in the mall, as well as a few free standing establishments around the mall," said the man claiming to be Mike.

"What if I didn't want to go to the mall," said Terrence.

"There are a few places that do deliver."

"Are they over there, at the mall?" Terrence motioned toward mall without actually looking at it, as if laying his eyes on it might taint his vision.

"Yes, would you like me to get you their numbers?"

"Is there anywhere to eat that isn't in the mall, or affiliated with the mall, or touching the mall?"

"Of course, there are plenty of places, but the mall has everything you could possibly need, and more. They even have a pharmacy, and a grocery store."

"Are any of them close? The places that aren't in the mall?"

"No," said Mike.

"Is there a vending machine?"

After devouring, three bags of processed cheese food filled pretzels and half a bottle of Absinthe, he knew that this would be no way for him to subsist while waiting for Andy.

"What do you mean you haven't left yet," said Terrence into the pay phone.

"Sorry things got kind of crazy at work," said Andy.

"Do you have the slightest inclination, what I am attempting to accomplish here?"

"Not really," said Andy. "I thought you were trying to go on a vacation and try to relax."

"That is just like you. You abandon me in Paris, now you abandon me here in some bizarre circle of hell. Do you realize that there is nothing to eat? All they have is a vending machine."

"I thought you were across the street from a mall."

"I am."

"Then why don't you go over there?"

"Why don't you fuck off?"

"Good luck getting home."

Terrence heard the line go dead. Terrence thought about calling some of his old friends from Detroit, but it had been so long since he had seen any of them, that he didn't even know if they were still there. Contacting his parents was not an option. He stared across the six lane divided highway at the mall, and walked back to his room. After another visit to the vending machine, the greasy pretzels dehydrated him, the processed cheese food gave him mud butt, and the Absinthe gave him the courage to explore the mall.

The divided highway cut across concrete landscape like a raging river. If there had been a crosswalk, Terrence might have considered using it, but this was an area that had developed around the mall over the past fifteen years. A crosswalk made as much sense as a boat launch. People didn't sail to the mall, so why bother? This same logic held true for the crosswalk as well. Terrence stood there and waited for a sign, some moment of convergence, when he cosmos would tell him in his innocent state that it would be all right to cross. A pair of BMWs sped by followed by a Mercedes and a Jaguar. Two large delivery trucks passed with large advertisements on them. Terrence thought about the absurd transparency of the marketing on them, and how it was so completely lost on him. Then he saw the Yugo and the baby shit orange 1980 two door Toyota Corolla. He knew this was the sign he had been waiting for. As Terrence staggered across, fearing that he might be either some insane panhandler, or over exuberant Shriner, cars ground to a halt. The drivers rolled down their windows and dangled dollar bills at Terrence.

Thirty-seven dollars richer, Terrence found himself in the mall. It had been a long time since he had been in an actual mall. In Santa Monica, Terrence would usually get most of what he needed on the Third Street Promenade, an approximation of an imagined main street, filled with chain stores, street performers, sun, and beautiful people. The outdoor nature of the Promenade hadn't prepared him of the claustrophobia he was experiencing in an aging Midwestern mall. He felt like he was in Dawn of the Dead. Here he saw them. Hopeless and bloated, they slowly wandered from store to store, eating and purchasing items they neither needed nor wanted. Signs led them like cattle from one "Sale" to the next, as soft music lifted their self-esteem and fed their need to consume. This was where Terrence was needed; this was where the liberation would be unleashed.

Terrence was shocked at how easy it was to rent a kiosk at the mall. He had developed a back-story and falsified a business license. He was prepared to show them over three different forms of identification. All the mall management really wanted was to insure his availability of funds. After that Terrence was assigned a space on the third floor next a Piercing Palace. This franchise specialized in, "everything but the ear", but usually found themselves piercing the ears of underage girls, and boys, who faked their parent's permission. The bored owner, Bob or Crüeböy72 to his friends, would file the forged note, pierce the kid, and ask them to fuck off.

Bob was not very excited about the kiosk next to him being rented. He really hoped that whoever rented it, would have the decency to either be cool, or at a minimum have the ability to shut the fuck up. Last Christmas, a woman with more money than sense decided that she needed to express herself by creating what she claimed was art. She, being busy creating, staffed her kiosk with her bored teen-age daughter, who excelled at being a stereotype. She was the poster child for the young, wealthy, and bored. She spent hour after hour screaming into her cell phone, bemoaning her lot in life to other members of the growing throng of the useless. It became too much for Bob. The cell phone was crushed, using one of the ugly bronze vases that her mother had created. The mother promptly moved to a more reputable mall, in a more exclusive suburb. Bob was asked by mall management to be nice.

He tried, he always tried, but sometimes people were just douche bags. Looking at the pretty Arab kid in the suit, he envisioned the nightmare that could come.

"What ya selling?" said Bob.

"I am selling nothing," said Terence. His slightly crooked smile was beginning to irritate Bob.

"Please tell me that you aren't one of those douche bags who claims to not sell anything, because the product sells itself," said Bob. "Because there is nothing that sells itself, not even pussy. Think about it- half this mall is devoted to the packaging and marketing of pussy, from the foundation to the lace panties. So tell me, what the hell has been invented on this planet better than pussy."

"No," said Terrence. "I really am not selling anything."

Now this asshole was beginning to get offensive, thought Bob. He might have to give him a pass if he ends up being gay, but if he is just being an asshole, he might have to pound him.

"So you just decided to rent a kiosk in this crap mall for shits and giggles?" said Bob.

"What kind of an asshole would do that?" said Terrence. "No, I'm here to try to change the world."

"Perfect," said Bob. "Just what the world needs another God damned tree hugger. Well let me tell you right now, that I have no intention of signing your damned petitions."

"Fantastic," said Terrence. "Because, I don't have any petitions. Just this." Terrence held out a sample cup, which held a milky green substance.

"Is it a heath drink?" said Terrence.

"Nope."

"Mouthwash?"

"Nope."

"Is it dangerous?"

"Very."

Bob, who was really beginning to dislike this kid, thought that he had two courses of action. He could hit the kid, or he could drink the stuff, and then hit the kid. Bob knew that the way the kid said "very" was clearly a challenge. Bob knew he would need to establish that he was going to be the Alpha in this relationship.

Bob grabbed he sample cup and downed it, then world tilted. Not by much, but by just enough to make him smile.

"That's not bad, could I have another?" said Bob.

"Sure, but then I have to start handing out the samples," said Terrence.

"Can I help?" said Bob.

The first day they only handed out a handful of samples, but more than made up for it by splitting another bottle of mouthwash between them. The next day, word had gotten around, and there were quite a few people asking for Terrence's drink. Terrence had few rules, first, no kids were allowed, but anyone sixteen and over were. Seconds were allowed, but only after everyone in line had had his or her first. There would be no shoving in line, no cutting, and anyone talking on a cell phone in line would be kicked in the nut sack. That last one was Bob's, but Terrence didn't mind.

The samples went so quickly, that he was grateful for Bob's help. It was a wonderful success, until the minor riot that broke out in the Una's Undies, which spilled out into the Pretzel Pagoda, and eventually finished in the Republic of Fashion.

As the finger pointing began, someone thought to blame Terrence. Mall security was quick to try out their new Tasers, both Bob and Terrence went down quickly and were taken to a quiet room near the mall offices.

Bob, being Bob, was quickly released to the local police. Terrence, being Arab, was a much more complex issue. The local police thought that it might be a federal issue. However, on the Federal level, no one was quite certain if it should fall to the ATF, TSA, CIA, NSA, or the Department of Homeland Security. It was this confusion that caused Terrence to be left alone in a locked cramped room, handcuffed to a conference table with the remaining eight bottles of Absinthe, the only evidence against him.

Downing the first bottle was easy. He had been drinking Absinthe to excess for long enough that he really didn't give it much thought. About halfway through the fourth bottle was when Terrence's hallucinations began to intensify.

He felt his body floating out into the mall. The shoppers were mechanically walking into and out of each store. Peering at the sale rack, occasionally someone would make a purchase. Often they just walked aimlessly, directed by the large marketing campaigns, which enticed them to explore shop after shop. Until, one of the stores actually began to eat the customers. The blood splattered across the other shoppers, who enjoyed this new form of marketing. This wasn't a sale, this was actual painful death facing them, and they couldn't refuse how imaginative it was. Terrence tried to do something to stop them entering. The Store would occasionally burp and out would come a fashionably dressed, but morbidly obese amalgam of the many people who had gone in before. Then this new creature would walk into and out of the shops, constantly become larger, but also more nondescript. The face became blank, more generic.

The next morning, Terrence was found in the room, naked, screaming, with eight empty bottles of mouthwash. The trial was brief. Terrence had to agree to not sue the mall, or the other agencies involved, and he would be able to avoid jail time, but he would have to agree to four hundred hours of community service. Terrence agreed.

For Terrence, his world was now permanently tilted.

Lies

Harold stared at Terrence for a long time. The small outdoor cafe was usually adrift with hipsters, the wealthy and the beautiful. But, this being mid morning on a Thursday, even the wait staff was fine with the Arab guy and the dude in the hospital gown taking a highly coveted seat. Harold and Terrence were seated and then promptly ignored. This was one of the many ways the place kept up its air of exclusivity. Harold took advantage of this time to stare deeply into Terrence's eyes.

"You hate me don't you," said Terrence.

"No," said Harold.

"Who the hell do you think you are to judge me?" said Terrence.

"I'm an alien from just left of galactic center, here to observe the human race and a programmed need to find validation in belonging to various social structures," said Harold. "Would you allow me to observe you?"

"Are you just going to sit there and stare at me?"

"Sometimes," said Harold.

"No, you won't learn anything about the human race like that," said Terrence. "You need to experience it. You know, like traveling to another country. You need to walk away from the tour and lose the phrase book."

"We already tried that."

"Maybe you were watching the wrong people."

"How could I have been watching the wrong people?" said Harold. "There is only one type of dominant species on this planet."

"Not really, not if all of you guys were sent here to assimilate and observe, and you said that is was supposed to look like a new baby boom, with all of your kind arriving," said Terrence.

"Go, on," said Harold.

"You have millions of aliens all showing up, at roughly the same time. All of them conditioned to want to fit in. Statistically speaking, the probability of you running into other aliens is highly likely."

"And since we all felt such a tight need to belong and be accepted, we became a group unto ourselves."

"All these years, that means that you haven't been observing us, you've just been observing each other! Isn't that remarkable!"

"So do you really think that I'm telling the truth?"

"Be careful how you ask a question like that."

"Why?"

"The obvious answer would be because you might not like the answer. I hardly know you, how do I know if I answer that question truthfully that you might not grab a steak knife off the table and plunge it into my chest?"

"So, I shouldn't ask?

"I would never tell anyone that the pursuit of knowledge was not a fruitful endeavor. What I said was you should make certain that you are very clear in asking the questions that you mean to ask. Here you are asking me if I think that the fact that you are an alien is the Truth. The Truth with a capital T. That would infer that there was some kind of a separate objective entity looking down upon us and impartially observing events. Whenever anything happens, anywhere, there will always be at least one highly biased individual observing the event, usually more. Be wary of anyone who comes even close to telling you that they are the sole individual who can actually be impartial. Every individual brings every second of their lives with them to the table, and experiences it through the stained glass of their own subjective. Therefore, do I think that it is the Truth, capital T, that you are an alien energy signature hiding out in the pudgy frame of a bigoted white dude? Of course not, but only because I believe that there is no such thing as THE Truth, with a capital T. But, I do believe that you feel that it is your Truth."

"Thank you," said Harold.

"I need to pee," said Terrence, as he rose from the table.

Harold watched him as he walked into the coffee shop. Looking across the small square in the center of the village, the green of the grass looked lush against the red and blue flashing lights. Six police cruisers converged on the coffee shop. Small children came running to see, as mothers and nannies grabbed them and ran in the opposite direction. The officers exited their cruisers and pointed their guns at Harold. Harold smiled and waved. One of the men exited the cruiser in a black suit holding a megaphone, in spite of being twenty feet from Harold's table; he switched the power on with a loud whine of feedback.

"Sir, I need you to get down," said the man with the megaphone.

"Why?" asked Harold.

"We have reports of an Arab in the vicinity," said the officer. "We suspect that he kidnapped a patient from the hospital."

"Oh, dear," said Harold. "Well I haven't seen anyone from the hospital today, but me. And I definitely haven't seen anyone being kidnapped."

"No?" said the office.

"No," said Harold. "I wanted to leave before my wife showed up, so my friend helped me."

"Are you at this moment under any duress?"

"No, I just don't want to deal with my wife," said Harold.

"So you haven't been kidnapped?"

"No."

"Oh," said the man with the megaphone. "That is a bit of a disappointment. Here I was hoping that we might actually be onto something."

"Nope."

"I mean I've got the megaphone, the rest of the guys here they were really excited. I think this is actually the first time Joey has gotten to wear his bulletproof vest. I know it's the first time I've gotten to call the Department of Homeland Security."

"How was that?"

"Say what you will, but they were shockingly helpful, and really rather chipper the entire time I was on the phone with them. Have you seen any Arabs?"

"To be honest, I've been having so much fun with my new friend Terrence, I haven't been paying that much attention."

"And Terrence?"

"He's from Detroit."

"Never mind then," said the man with the megaphone. "Hope we didn't ruin your lunch."

"Sorry I couldn't be more help," said Harold.

The man with the megaphone signaled the other officers to stand down. They got into their cruisers and left.

"So, what would you like to do first?" said Terrence as he returned to the table.

"I need some clothing," said Harold. "But, then I think we need to get out of here. I get the feeling that it might not be the best of places for us."

Ami was not in the mood. She was not in the mood for any of it. She, to be perfectly frank, was really hoping that the world would just hurry up and implode. The hospital losing her husband pushed her to the edge. The police finding him, and then letting him go, pushed her over it. She raced back in the SUV. The front mangled enough to show that she had been in a bit of an accident. She tried to smile as she drove past her own face on the signs in front of the houses she was trying to sell.

The bursting of the housing bubble was going to be an opportunity for her. It had to be. She pulled into the bank parking lot, and ignored the sign expressly reserving the parking spot for the handicapped. A young man, who was about to tell her that she couldn't park there, glanced at her withering gaze and thought the better of it.

Walking into the bank, she disregarded the "sign in sheet" and walked back to a man in a suit. This was no time for bullshit rules and waiting in line. This was a desperate moment of shocking momentum, it needed to be respected, and addressed.

"My husband has lost his mind, and I fear that he might drain my account," she told him. "You need to cancel his ATM card."

"Did you sign in?" asked the man in the suit.

"No, and I don't have time for this, I need you freeze his ATM card."

"Was your husband's ATM card stolen?"

"No."

"Has he been declared unfit by a court of law?"

"No."

"Then, I'm afraid, that there is little I could do for you right now."

"You don't understand, he was supposed to be dead," said Ami.

"You wanted you husband to be dead?"

"Not exactly wanted, but it would have made everything so much easier. All I want is for him to not be able to take all of the money out of our accounts."

"Well there is the daily withdrawal limit."

"Can I close the accounts?"

"Well since it is a joint account, I would need you to actually-"

Ami didn't let him finish, there wasn't any need; she walked out of the bank.

Terrence and Harold stood behind the large home that Harold shared with his wife.

"Why don't you just go in through the front door?" said Terrence.

"Because, I can't live here anymore," said Harold. "If I don't live here anymore, then I need to break in."

"Why?" said Terrence.

"I just do," said Harold.

"Well, could I just head in through the back door?"

"Good luck getting in, Ami has four deadbolts on that door, and never leaves the house without locking each of them twice. She's mildly OCD."

"It's open, and that kid is staring at you."

HoJo came out back to see what was going on. His shock from seeing his father was really only outweighed by the terror of seeing an Arab.

"You are supposed to be in school right now," said Harold.

"You're supposed to be dead," said HoJo. "Why are you here with a terrorist?"

"He's not a terrorist, well he was a terrorist, but a nice terrorist," said Harold. "With a sense of humor. He's from Detroit."

"Did he kidnap you?" said HoJo.

"Why would I kidnap him?" said Terrence. "Do you think I collect pudgy white people? Should I get you for my collection?"

"Don't scare him," said Harold.

"What are you doing here?" said HoJo.

"This might be a little difficult to explain to you," said Harold. "But, I need to leave."

"You're abandoning us?" said HoJo.

"Not exactly aban-" said Harold.

"That's awesome," said HoJo. "Did you come back to trash the place or anything like that?"

"No, I just came back to grab some clothes," said Harold.

"Come on in!" said HoJo.

HoJo couldn't believe his luck. Here he was on the verge of his father abandoning him and running off with an Arab. This could easily be some kind of homosexual terrorist tale of forbidden love. If he played this right, it could easily lead to Kelly letting him touch her.

Harold and Terrence walked in through the back door.

"This might be a little difficult for you to understand," said Harold. "But, I have had a recent revelation, and I need to go and experience your planet. I'm an alien."

"Good for you," said HoJo. "I think that is just great, long overdue really."

"You understand?" said Harold.

"Why wouldn't I?" said HoJo. "But, you need to hurry. Mom should be home soon."

Harold rushed up stairs to stuff a duffle bag full of clothes.

"You don't seem all that broken up about your dad leaving," said Terrence.

"And you don't seem to be too torn up about taking advantage of a stroke victim," said HoJo.

"Hey, good talk," said Terrence, as Harold came back down the stairs, the duffle bag trailing behind him.

"You blow all our money and I will find you," said HoJo.

Harold took a long look at HoJo.

"Are you sure you're all right with this?" said Harold.

"Sure I am, don't forget to take the car," said HoJo. "That way you can get a head start."

Harold smiled at HoJo, and with Terrence behind him they left. The small sports sedan screeched out of the driveway and onto the quiet street. As it sped away, HoJo grabbed the china hutch and pushed it.

Ami knew that Harold had a vindictive streak in him, but seeing the way that he had trashed the house, was inexcusable. The things that HoJo reported he had said to him, that really was just plain wrong. The China Hutch, the sofa, the urine on the carpet, what kind of self respecting human being does something like that? HoJo had cried so much, his eyes were red. Ami didn't want Harold back. He could stay gone for all she cared. But, she was going to make the little son of a bitch pay.

Donuts

Nazarene, Illinois had been founded on three principles: One was to live one's life with strict adherence to God's laws, as set out in the Bible, Second, was that there wasn't much that conversation over a cup of coffee and a donut couldn't solve, Third, no brown people. In its early days the mayor/reverend of Nazarene, Ignatius F. Watch, saw the birth of a beautiful idea. However, as time went on, as with many new and shiny things, the tarnish began to show.

The small religious town didn't seem to be growing into the Mecca of southern Illinois that they knew it could be, in fact the town itself was so far in debt, that to balance the books, Ignatius lied. He didn't fluff the numbers, he didn't creatively account for the losses the city had, he downright lied, and had his brother, the city Treasurer, his cousins on the city board, and his wife lie with him.

There were prayer meetings hoping that it might help solve the problems of the small aspiring utopia. But, with no industry, failing agriculture, and no draw for tourists; it was only a matter of time before the small village would have to declare bankruptcy.

When it was announced that a high speed interstate would be coming through the area, just a mere twenty five miles east of the town, Ignatius knew this was the salvation they had been praying for. For three days he fasted and prayed, preemptively thanking God for his divine intervention on the behalf of the reverend/mayor and the good and pious residents of Nazarene. It was the afternoon of the third day that the angel came to him.

Ignatius' prayer room was modest compared to many of the others in the village. The paint on the wall was eggshell. There had been much discussion on the proper color of the prayer room. There were a few purists in town that insisted that the room needed to be pure white. Ignatius argued that if the good Lord were to send anyone down to speak to you, their heavenly light would bounce off the walls, giving anyone one in that pure white room a sunburn. Granted, if the good Lord did need to talk to you, you'd probably have other worries than one's skin care.

Regardless, as the angel spoke to Ignatius, he was pleased that he went with the eggshell. What Ignatius didn't realize was that the voice he was hearing was not actually the voice of an angel, but rather was the result of a short in his new radio.

The reverend/mayor had always been fascinated by the radio. The fact that the radio, and the new invention television, could carry the words of individuals halfway across the world humbled him. This meant that the Good Word could travel far and wide. This also meant that other things could travel as well. To ensure that this not happen in his home, the reverend/mayor would hang a cross over the radio. This did little to no good; there were still stories of atrocities as well at filth that would come spewing forth. Ignatius returned six radios, fearing that he couldn't find one that would play the right type of things.

The city he traveled to purchase it was just over the state line, and quite a trek. The shopkeeper tried to explain that there was nothing that he personally could do regarding the content the radio could receive. It was possible to change the station, and find stations that the reverend/mayor might like, but hanging a cross from the radio would not do any good. This didn't stop him from requesting a replacement.

The small radio shop had three employees. The only one who hadn't tried to explain the issue to the right honorable reverend/mayor was Ezekiel. He was elected to be the one to speak to Ignatius when they saw his truck pull up in front of the shop. Ezekiel was the newest of the employees, brought on as someone with a good deal of knowledge of the new television sets. He would be both their resident expert and repairman. But, as the others left on lunch break to avoid dealing with the reverend/mayor and his insanity, Ezekiel cornered the owner and asked permission to have some fun with the reverend/mayor.

"Hello sir, and welcome to Pete's Radio Emporium," having some trouble with your radio?" said Ezekiel, sounding as sincere as he could.

"Yes, this will be the seventh one I have had to return," said Ignatius.

"What seems to be the problem?"

"Well, in spite of my attempts to the contrary this machine continues to spout the word of the devil."

"And what, precisely, have you done so far?"

"Well I hung a cross from it, and I prayed by it."

"That's it?" said Ezekiel. "You will have to forgive me for saying so, but I sure am happy that you aren't a preacher."

"Why do you say that?"

"Well if you're willing to give up that quickly on something as simple as a radio, I wouldn't want you dealing with something as complex as my soul."

"Really?"

"Of course, I mean if you think about it where does real change occur?"

"In the soul."

"And where is that?"

"In here," said Ignatius, pointing to his chest.

"If you were a preacher would you give up on a sinner after hanging a cross around his neck and a prayer?"

"No."

"You would try to save him, change him from the inside out. Save his soul."

"Are you telling me that I should do something to the inside of the radio? But, the other gentleman said that it would void the warranty."

"So happy you ain't a preacher," said Ezekiel. "If you try to save a soul does that void the warranty? Let's see about finding you a replacement."

"No, sir," said Ignatius, as he turned and walked back to his truck with his radio.

When he got home he removed the back of the radio, sprinkled it with holy water, and hung a metal cross inside. It was this combination, which caused the bright flash and shorted out the radio; causing it to turn on, pick up a television broadcast, a radio commercial for a coffee shop, and an evangelist from over the border.

"I don't mean to say that I am a doubting man by nature," said Ignatius, as he knelt in his prayer room. "Personally, I think that Thomas should have been as vilified as Judas. I think one of the smartest things they did was keep his book out of yours. But, I do have to say that I am having a crisis here. The town, it can't keep going on like this. I know I've sinned, I know I've lied to my flock. But, that was only for them; so that they would keep going, and we could continue to do your work. I just need a hand here, Jesus. How the hell are we going to do this? How can we keep going?"

"The proposed interstate-best donut you've ever - praise Jesus!"

Ignatius knew this was the answer.

Borrowing heavily, the First Nazarene Donut Hole was built. Daily prayer services were held inside the Donut Hole, to cause the interstate to come closer, if not through, the town. Not only didn't the interstate come any closer, but ironically, it was diverted an additional fifteen miles away. The nearest exit was a full fifty-six miles from Nazarene. Then, in a cruel twist of fate; a chemical used in making the asphalt found its way into the water supply of Nazarene, rendering all of the men sterile.

Broke and barren, the town of Nazarene continued to meet at the Donut Hole, as the residents slowly died off. Thirty years after the death of the last original resident, the Porn Tycoon Arnold Zimmerman purchased the entire town on a whim and turned the First Nazarene Donut Hole into a strip club/coffee house.

It was here that Harold found himself studying Terrence.

"Do you find it very relaxing to have strippers while having coffee and donuts?" said Harold, who had a large notebook with him. The pages were well worn and full of his notes and observations.

"No, I wouldn't say relaxing," said Terrence. "Mildly exploitative."

"Then why did you bring me here?" said Harold.

"Well this is one of those bizarre places you hear about and always mean to go," said Terrence. "You know what I mean. You hear all about these weird homages, collections, or bizarre festivals all over the States, but you never get around to seeing them. These are the places where real America can be found. America is mildly exploitative."

"Well at least the donuts are good," said Harold.

"And I have to say that they brew a mean cup of coffee," said Terrence.

"Thank you," said the nude woman on stage with the inflatable dinosaur.

"You're a very good dancer," said Harold.

"That is sweet of you," said the woman. "Ya'll want anything else, or should I just get you the check."

"Actually, could you direct me to the restroom," said Terrence.

The woman pointed with the dinosaur, then continued dancing across the stage. Terrence walked by truckers all sitting and drooling over donuts and the dancer. However, at the end of the hallway was a large rectangular poster. On that poster was a green female spirit, in all her art deco glory. Around the woman in large letters were the words "Old Absinthe House – New Orleans". It was at this moment that Terrence had his first really substantive flashback. The world tilted, in the opposite direction, and Terrence smiled.

Harold closed his eyes and began rubbing them with gentle pressure. The light behind his eyelids exploded. Over the bar was a large television, the volume turned to a dull mumble. Harold could just make out what they were saying on the television. There was a discussion going on regarding the first Individuality™ convention to be held in New Orleans. There in New Orleans, would be the largest gathering the world had ever seen of a group of individuals desperate to find a sense of belonging. Harold thought of the millions of Individuality™ users, and realized that they were just like him. What else would cause people to obsess over belonging to an imaginary community? Harold knew he could help them. Harold needed to go to New Orleans.

KAPOW!

Madam Leveaux's Comics Emporium and Palace of Voodoo, was a simple shop in the Quarter. The cedar planks that made up the floor creaked with the years of expansion from humidity, and the warping from floods. It smelled slightly of mildew and incense. One side of the long and narrow shop was covered with expensive back issues of comic books. Tamika Mourningwood (a.k.a. Madam Leveaux) prided herself on her near encyclopedic knowledge of comic books and comic book prices. She marveled at the art, the stories, and the social commentary. There was not one comic book on the wall that she hadn't personally read, inspected, and priced herself. She had slowly built herself a regional reputation for one of the best comic book stores in the entire Southeast. She loved that.

The other side of the shop was dedicated to, what most people referred to as her "gift". This "gift" is what attracted the tourists. Tamika found it more often than not got in the way of important things, like new comic book day.

Tamika stood at the counter putting together the pull boxes for the next day; meticulously placing the comic book into a bag and board before placing it into the pull box. After seven years she had 99% of her regulars' pull lists memorized.

"Excuse me," said the voice behind her.

Tamika let out a long slow sigh. Behind her was nothing more than a wall of valuable vintage comics.

"I said excuse me," reiterated the voice.

"Not today thank you," said Tamika.

"What?" said the voice. "Not today? Do you expect the universe to schedule everything around our availability? Who the hell do you think you are?"

Tamika turned to find she was staring at the cover of World's Finest Comics #11. Usually the cover had three well-known superheroes on it tending a victory garden to help with the war effort. Tamika had always liked that cover; it showed the earnestness of the golden age comic books perfectly. This cover didn't sport Nazis being pummeled, Japanese plains being ripped apart; it showed something that any kid could help out with. That was why she placed the thousand-dollar price tag on it. She knew it was only worth half that on a good day, but it was one of her favorites. However, right now she was ready to dump the damned thing in the trash. The youngest super hero on the comic book was looking directly at her.

"Today is new comic book day," she said to the boy on the cover. "I don't have time for this. I thought we understood that."

"Don't you take that tone with me," said the boy on the cover. As the figure on the cover of the comic book began to talk, it moved with the jerky motions of a flipbook.

"Fine," said Tamika. "I'm very sorry, but could we please do this tomorrow."

"No, Miss Mourningwood," said the boy. "There is a storm coming, and you need to prepare."

"A storm coming?" said Tamika, suppressing a laugh. "What do you think this is, a Stephen King novel?"

"Change is coming, and you had better prepare yourself."

"How many other clichés are you going to have to blurt out before you understand that I don't want this right now. I am not going to be the little old Creole woman sitting on the front porch telling people what to do. I have a comic book store to run."

"You leave us no choice, Miss Morningwood," said the boy.

"No, wait!" she said.

Her mind flooded with images, sounds and emotions of the future. She saw what was coming. She wiped the tears from her eyes, and then passed out on the floor. This was what always happened when the spirits bombarded her like that. She would be out for at least forty-five minutes. She made a mental note to burn that comic book.

Act Two:

Geraldine and the Art of Listening

Inception

For decades, scientists have been scanning the universe for any sign of intelligent life. As of yet, their fruitless search has been met by silence.

The universe is roughly 13.7 billion years old.

Scientists cannot agree on the actual size of the universe, but do agree that it is very large and expanding. They believe that the universe is full of dark matter. Strange matter that causes the universe to actually be more massive than it should be.

The weight of the universe is suspected to be 100 trillion, trillion, trillion, trillion tons.

Therefore, the universe is a petulant, fat, adolescent that continues to stuff itself with empty calories, and really just doesn't want to talk about it.

Stanton "Stan" Friedman and Hanna Cohn both worked for the United States Space Program. Not the poster child program "NASA" put together to distract the public, but the real space program. The USSP operated on an undisclosed Air Force base somewhere in Northern Florida. It was close enough to Cape Canaveral to not attract unwanted attention, but far enough away that they were clearly independent.

Stan and Hanna met at the University of Chicago. This was when the University was the center of the scientific world; where the early atomic tests were taking place, as was groundbreaking research on Dr. Albert Hoffman's synthesis of lysergic acid. This led to an environment, fueled by frenetic jazz, heroic amounts of LSD-25, the splitting of the atom, and math.

Stan loved solving complex mathematical problems while consuming LSD. For Stan, it caused his mind to see the limits of conventional computations, as well as their potential. He could see a complex mathematical problem, not as two-dimensional scratches on a page, but as three-dimensional puzzles, with a myriad of real world applications. It was while on a dose of LSD, listening to the Lou Sacco Orchestra, that Stan developed the concept of proton acceleration to create thrust.

Hanna also enjoyed consuming LSD. She also loved to design complex machinery, while altered. Nothing was more entertaining to her than finding some obscure scientific concept and designing a device to not only help explain the concept, but also have a practical application of it.

Hanna discovered Stan's idea of a proton acceleration system at a party. She found a piece of paper that Stan had been scribbling on most of the night. So inspired with the idea, she spent the weekend with a box of crayons, designing the first practical proton acceleration drive. She placed the plans on a community board in Stan's dorm.

Stan saw it, as he was coming down off the purest batch of LSD the chemistry lab had cooked to date. There on the message board in full Technicolor glory was his idea. Not only would it work, but also it could be built inexpensively, with materials that were on hand in the physics lab. Stan took down the blueprints, and after drinking a large glass of orange juice, scrawled a note to Hanna. It stated simply:

Who are you?

This was how Stan began his search for Hanna. Stan reasoned that there were only a few places that someone as brilliant as Hanna could hide. He knew that if he kept his eyes open, he would find her. After the first month he began to panic. Stan began placing cryptic messages on various boards around school. This took up much of his time. The remainders of his days were not filled with class work, but rather supervising the building of the test vehicle.

Stan had assembled a small group of friends to assist with the build. Ironically, this group included a mousy friend of a friend, who Stan found hopelessly attractive, Hanna.

Hanna found Stan not only phenomenally easy to talk to, but was shocked how much fun she had communicating with him. They found a myriad ways to communicate with each other, verbal, non-verbal, mathematically, abstractly. They did this so well, that Hanna assumed that they were dating. Stan enjoyed Hanna and thought she was breathtaking. However, since he hadn't received a response to his many posts on the community bulletin boards across campus, he began to idolize the mysterious woman who had designed his drive system.

Hanna thought the notes he left were a sweet and an elaborate way for him to flirt. Whenever she would make a modification to her original blueprint, Stan would rail and scream that no one should ever play with the obvious perfection he found in her work. Then, after given a moment to see what she had changed, he would praise her for her brilliance.

"How did you think of compensating for inertia with a dampening field, negating most of the gravitational pull," said Stan.

"It just came to me while I was listening to an old Louis Jordan album," said Hanna. "Right after 'Nobody Here But us Chickens', I was thinking of how to improve the thrust, but thought why not just try to reduce gravity?"

"It's brilliant, just brilliant," said Stan. "But, try not to do it again. Someone very remarkable made these plans, and for some strange reason has entrusted me to oversee their implementation. What would happen if she were to come here one day and discover that someone more brilliant than her has been improving upon her original designs?"

"I guess I would be flattered," she said.

"As well she should be, but please don't do it again." Hanna found this flattering. The rest of their friends saw what was going on and thought it was kind of strange.

The first two test flights of the new vessel worked flawlessly, that evening Stan and Hanna flew to the moon and back. However, on the third flight a missile clipped the vessel and the ship crashed in the southern Nevada Desert, near a small air force base. The missile hadn't actually been aimed at them; it was just a simple missile test. Stan and Hanna survived the crash, but were immediately arrested.

Hanna and Stan were taken from their cell, and placed in an interrogation room. It looked much like their cell, just larger with a table and chairs. Behind the table sat two men in black suits, one was operating a reel-to-reel tape recorder. Hanna and Stan stood before them.

"I would like to lodge a formal complaint," said Hanna. Stan stared at her, surprised by her new boldness.

"And that would be?" asked man operating the reel to reel.

"I was disappointed that our cell didn't have proper bars," said Hanna. "You know, like in the movies."

"You wished we put you in a movie cell?" said the other man.

"Well, I've never been arrested before, and you kind of have this image in your head how it's going to go," said Hanna.

"I'm sorry it has been a weird day for us," said Stan. "We've never been arrested before."

"Getting arrested is weird, but launching yourself into orbit is normal?" said the man operating the reel to reel.

"Oh, no we didn't make it into orbit," said Stan. "We made it to the moon and back. Twice."

"How long did that take you?" asked the other man.

"Just this evening," said Hanna.

"Who designed the drive system?"

"It was based on a theory of mine," said Stan.

"I made the first practical design," said Hanna.

"You did?" said Stan, as the realization washed over him. Before him was the exact person he had been trying to find. Promptly ignoring the inquest, Stan kissed Hanna for the first time.

The men in black suits knew putting Stan and Hanna to work building the Photon Acceleration Drive for the USSP was the next logical step. It was this drive that led the first manned mission to Mars in 1958, and the establishment of the first Martian colony. Stan and Hanna were instrumental in the terraforming of Io, the mining of the ice mines of Europa, and the exploration of most of the outer spiral. The government loved how well they worked, as well as how little they asked in return. Granted, there were the vast amounts of psychotropic drugs that they consumed, but they were prolific in producing vast numbers of advances. It took longer than many had expected for them to marry, but this had little to do with desire, and much more to do with their schedule.

They never forgot how lucky they were to not only have found each other, and together became part of a much larger universe than they previously knew existed. This was one of those remarkable moments where people actually find their perfect match. They were, for lack of a better cliché, soul mates. They communicated with each other in such wonderful and remarkable ways. Working on a complex program, each would hide small love notes in the computer code, or deep within a logarithm, and even in an equation. It was remarkable that they communicated with each other so completely.

They shared a modest house in what appeared to be a planned community, but in reality was part of an Air force base that housed some of the country's best and brightest. To say that it was a bit of a strange place to live would be an understatement. It often resembled an MIT party, with huge amounts of psychedelic drugs. Other times it resembled an MIT party, with huge amounts of drugs from the future. But, for all intents and purposes, it also resembled a fifties suburban paradise. The homes were well kept, the lawns well manicured. The sidewalks were safe, and it was one of the few places left in America, where kids were allowed to play outside, without fear for their safety.

This is why when the issue of children was broached, it became a sound conclusion that Hanna and Stan, try to have a child. A large amount of incense was burned. A few tantric prayers were mumbled over the bed, and before the second hit of LSD set in, they made love. This was not the first time that Stan and Hanna had sex. They actually had sex quite often, but this was the first time that they were having sex with the intent of conceiving a child. This, to them, clearly made all the difference.

Geraldine Schrödinger Peaceblossom was born on a frigid December day in 1973. Stan used his latest terraforming experiment to treat everyone to a perfect spring day, for a day and a half the sun smiled down on Geraldine. Hanna and Stan agreed that they would name their child, in accordance of the traditions of their Martian friends. The first name had to be one that was passed down from the maternal great grandmother, but the rest of the name would be bestowed as a blessing for the child. Hanna liked the idea of giving Geraldine a last name that reflected both the time when she was born, but also her desire that she live an exemplary life. Schrödinger was dropped in, hoping that she would be brilliant, and know how to tell a good dick joke.

Unbeknownst to her genius parents Geraldine was born with a unique ability, the ability to listen. Which although doesn't sound all that remarkable, listening is a skill which individuals have to learn as they grow. A group of children placed together in a small room will quickly begin to scream, for no other reason to see who can be the loudest. In marriage counseling sessions across the globe, therapists plead with their patients to actually listen to each other; hearing what their partner is saying rather than what they want to hear. Morning talk show hosts are paid millions to perfect how to look as if they are sincerely listening. People in casual conversations across the globe feign interest to appear polite, but usually have their mind on a completely different agenda. This sounds rude, until one realizes that no one is really listening.

Geraldine, however, was born with the ability to listen, and listen to such a superb degree that not only could she hear what people were actually saying; she could also hear what people meant to say. For a young girl, this made for a very confusing world. Any time someone would speak, she would listen. Hearing what was said, then, as a faint echo, she would hear what they actually meant to say.

This led to strange moments when her parents would take her grocery shopping. A woman complaining about a product would become a woman who felt powerless in her current situation, and this was one of the only moments that she could actually give a voice to her desperate fears. This was why she sounded so shrill. A man complaining about the price of a gallon of milk would actually be expressing his fears for his future employment. Her parents being scientists and hippies usually said what they meant, and meant what they said. That lasted until Geraldine turned three.

Reaction

Stan and Hanna had been told repeatedly by Geraldine's pediatrician that there was absolutely nothing for them to worry about. That all children develop differently. Some children were early walkers, some crawl for a bit longer. Some children learn to talk early, and babble constantly. Others take their time until they actually have something to say. But, the pediatrician would stress, be careful what you wish for, because often once children start talking they rarely stop. This was before her three-year check up.

Hanna and Stan both feared that they had done something wrong, but were quickly lulled into a silent fear that there might be something wrong with their daughter. There seemed to be nothing wrong with her hearing. She always listened and was very attentive. She seemed like a happy and intelligent child, except that she didn't speak. She would laugh, smile, and even on very rare occasions, she would cry, but she had never said a word.

At her three-year wellness check the pediatrician admitted that this might be an issue. This admission had very striking, but also very different effects on Stan and Hanna.

Hanna became wildly defensive. She loved her daughter deeply, how anyone could possibly infer that his or her child was in any way shape or form defective was obscene. Why they couldn't just let her develop they way she was going to develop, became a constant point of contention between Hanna and the doctors, but more seriously with Stan.

Stan, however, dealt with his guilt by blaming their lifestyle. His daughter's deficiency in speech must have been a by-product of their drug use. And if Hanna would just take the time to listen to what he was knew was the problem, maybe they wouldn't be arguing so much all the time.

Geraldine was listening. She couldn't stop listening. As her world around her upended itself, she tried to make sense of what was happening.

Stan rejected their previous lifestyle, swearing off drug use of any kind. He started a neighborhood watch, as well as a block association. Neither seemed necessary to Stan's neighbors, the neighborhood being on a secure secret military base. But, hearing what Stan and Hanna were dealing with, and being their friends, neighbors, colleagues and trip buddies, they played along.

The newly formed block association, quickly named Stan the president, because no one else wanted to deal with it. They also quickly approved Stan's block bylaws, which no one bothered to read. The officers on the base saw this as a welcome respite to the chaos that usually ruled.

Stan became obsessed with the minutiae of every day existence, and wanted to regulate and control anything he could. This stemmed from his feelings of hopelessness, and was a very honest response to what was going on around him. If anyone, other than Geraldine, had been listening to what Stan was desperate to admit, they might have been able to understand what the bylaws really were. Instead they rolled their eyes when they saw him measuring the height of their grass, checked the way they pulled into their garages, and who parked on the streets after dark. All he really needed was a hug and for someone to tell him it was going to be okay.

Ironically, Hanna, needing the same thing, threw herself into her work and drugs. Now that everyone was focused on Geraldine's lack of talking, Hanna quickly found ways to deflect their obsession with Geraldine's defects by praising her.

As test after test would prove inconclusive, they became grueling wastes of time for Hanna. Trying to find an escape from the long drives off base to see "experts", the mind numbing tedium of the myriad waiting rooms, she began talking to Geraldine. Now this was something that she already did as a dutiful mother to a small child. But, now Hanna began speaking to her as a confidant, a true and trusted friend, and, on occasion, a therapist. As her husband drifted further and further away, she discovered how easy Geraldine was to talk to.

With Stan's new obsession with their community, the burden of the housework and Geraldine fell to Hanna. Neither of which was a chore. Geraldine was growing into a confident, self-sufficient child. She would never speak, but if asked to perform a task, and had that task explained to her methodically, the task would easily be accomplished. Hanna had no real idea how to nag or be a pest to her daughter. Hanna for her part tried to never abuse this newfound willingness to assist.

Hanna also tried to find new and intense ways of frustrating Stan. This would often involve some strategically ignored piece of housework, combined with some activity that Stan used to enjoy, but now frowned upon, i.e. drugs.

This would lead to a series of heated arguments that would end with someone slamming something and someone else running out the back door. Stan was always very insistent that the back door be used. If the front door was used then people might see what was going on. And people shouldn't talk about him. At least he hoped they wouldn't talk about him. Hanna told him that he was an asshole and would slam any door she pleased, and then took a bong hit.

Geraldine watched as they argued, and saw something very different. Geraldine saw them communicating the way they once had. Telling each other, daily how much they cherished each other. They expressed their deep guilt about what had happened in their lives, and to their daughter. Sure there were other things said, but Geraldine focused on what they really wanted to say.

Hanna didn't hate having to spend the time she did with her daughter on testing days, she just hated the doctors. She could see in each of them her husband, and his bullshit obsession with the minutiae. This was why she would roll, and smoke, a heroically large joint. Hanna being a caring and loving mother would always insist that her daughter be in the front seat with her, especially when she was driving and smoking marijuana.

Geraldine loved testing days. Her mother was
open with her, the way she was feeling, the way life ?
were never a series of absolutes, but rather a patchwork of rea
good guesses. Eventually, the conversation would devolve into her
mother drawing. She would draw the most wonderful things,
designing new space ships, refining her design of the photon drive.
She was even beginning to work on her new Huon drive system,
where the space craft would move sideways through dimensions and
seem to appear at its destination a trillionth of a second before it
departed.

"This is going to be the next step," Hanna would say. "This
is what is going to keep us in touch with the rest of the universe. We
will be able to not only travel nearly infinite distances in the blink of
an eye, but we will also be able to send communication
instantaneously. We will be able to reach and connect with every
corner of the known universe, instead of trying to regulate it."

Geraldine knew what her father was trying to do; she could
hear his concern and guilt every time he pushed his wife further and
further away. She also knew what her mother was trying to do as
she retreated deeper and deeper into her drug use.

This was what many people who watch daytime television
would call a destructive cycle. In reality it was two people who were
feeling too guilty to feel that they had enough self worth to express
their true feelings.

"I really don't know," said Hanna, as the car narrowly missed
slamming into a large, red, parked car. "Your father is just such a

in lately. Do you know that he told me that I wasn't getting his shirts pressed well enough? Can you believe that? Like I'm his mother or something like that. I've got a job, too, an important one. If I can get the Huon drive working, do know what that will do for us? Isn't it wonderful? I do have to say that I do like the outer spiral. It really is shockingly beautiful out there. One day, I really do hope to take you. It will be remarkable. There is this one planet where the butterflies are the size of Volkswagens, and the sky is day glow green!"

Hanna took another long draw of the joint in her mouth and began drawing frantically on a piece of paper. The fact that she was driving didn't seem to matter. Luckily, they were only going five miles an hour when they struck the back of the Congressman Reverend Dinkel's car.

The Congressman Reverend Dinkel was a Baptist preacher turned politician, and with the support of his wife and three daughters, he waged a moral war across the state, which he pledged to bring to the Senate if elected in the fall. He wanted to put God back into God Bless America. He wanted to bring "us" back to Jesus. And seven other trite sound bites that he placed on buttons, billboards, and the back of benches across most of the state. He tried to steer clear of the more educated and "Jewish" parts of the state. The liberal godless media would twist his message, and use it to fuel a backlash. If he was going to make it into the Senate, he was going to need to make it on the merits of the rural voter. The salt of the earth, the people like him, who liked him. The declining morals he saw around him were shocking to someone of his moral fortitude. He would never describe himself as a homophobic zealot, as many of the local papers had, because he was deeply in love with his personal assistant, Joe. Not to say that there wasn't a good deal of self-loathing with the Reverend, but he wasn't truly homophobic.

Reverend Dinkel jumped from the large black car. He saw the woman behind the wheel of the car with the young girl next to her. He quickly stopped the torrent of expletives that were going to be raining from his mouth. The Congressman Reverend Dinkel took a long hard look at the car. He had a temper. It was one of those things that could get the best of him, especially if he had been drinking, which he had been.

An afternoon lunch with some supporters had not only led to a few extra martinis, but also made him late for his clandestine meeting with Joe. This was not a good time for a fender bender. In his head he counted to ten. Then he counted to ten thinking of his wife and daughter. Then he counted to ten thinking of his Joe's naked body. Finally he spoke.

"Oh dear this doesn't look like it's going to cost too much, do you?" he said, flashing his two hundred dollar smile at Hanna and Geraldine.

Hanna didn't like the look of him. And in her current state she was convinced that the man with the big smile, who looked like a game show host, wanted to kill her. She didn't know why, but here was a moment of fight or flight, which came over her and was magnified in such an extreme way that she looked at the

Congressman Reverend Dinkel and screamed. Hanna and Geraldine were never in any real danger. The two bored men in black suits sitting in the dark nondescript car behind them made sure of that. They were minders, just to make certain that nothing detrimental happened to one of America's top scientist.

"Ma'am," said the Reverend Dinkel, "Have you been injured? Would you like me to call the authorities?"

Why is he grinning so goddamned much? Thought Hanna. What the hell does he want from me?

Geraldine knew precisely what he wanted to do, but why he was saying it in such graphic detail to her mother was completely beyond her. She didn't understand much of what grownups did, let alone what grownups who didn't say what they meant nor meant what they said. But, now with the torrent of repressed sexual desire, paired with alcoholic rage, was giving Geraldine quite a lesson.

"Look," said the big glossy smile. "I am going to go now. I don't think the damage is great. The accident was clearly your fault. I'll slip my card through your window. I'm doing a rally tomorrow at the fairgrounds if your husband would like to discuss the accident. Is that alright?"

Hanna stared at the card that was stuck to the windshield under the windshield wiper. The man with the smile got into his car and drove off, waving and smiling the entire time. But, the Congressman Reverend Dinkel couldn't shake the feeling that Hanna could see through him. That she knew his secret, maybe even the child knew. That must be why they didn't say anything, they found his infidelity repulsive. This was often the way that the Congressman Reverend Dinkel felt after meeting someone outside of a controlled environment.

Hanna dismissed the appointment and drove back to the base, very carefully. Once home, she secured herself and Geraldine inside. She didn't even bother to clean the car seat, which she had wet.

Frank, the next-door neighbor came out to see what the screaming and crying was about. The car was dented, but no one seemed hurt. Geraldine even waved to him as Hanna rushed her into the house. Fred had always liked Geraldine. He wasn't so sure about Hanna, but Stan since his transformation was becoming quite the contentious neighbor.

Hanna thought Fred a stereotype, and until Stan had changed his ways, he had thought so as well. Now, being the head of the block association, Stan felt that he had his priorities straight, and could appreciate Fred for who he was, a swell neighbor.

Frank was still eyeing the car when Stan came home.

"Hi, Frank!" said Stan getting out of his car. "Is everything alright?"

"No it goddamned isn't," said Frank, as he took a swig from his beer. "Just look at it!"

"Is it the St. Augustine grass?" said Stan recalling their last discussion regarding the state of the lawn.

"No," said Frank. "Forget about that goddamned weed. There are far more serious issues at hand."

Back when Stan and Hanna were speaking, smoking, and fucking they would have games based around guessing what it was that Frank actually did on base.

"I'm sorry I'm not following."

"What ya gonna do?" said Frank.

"I don't know," said Stan. "I'm not even sure what you're talking about? Is it some other kind of weed?"

"No," said Frank, turning to Stan in a conspiratorial manner. "About the car. Now I know you're part of this whole younger generation, but lately you've seemed to really know what's good for you, and the community here. You're really starting to fit in here. And if you just let a thing like this slide."

"I'm sorry," said Stan. "I am just completely lost here. Is there something wrong?"

"Goddamnit!" said Frank, taking another sip from his can of beer. "She didn't even tell you. When she came home, I should have told her to call you right away. You don't want things like this to wait. When things like this wait, it ends up getting ugly."

"Could you just tell me what the hell you're talking about?"

"No reason to take that tone with me, I'm not the one who cracked up your car, she is!"

Stan ran toward the house.

Frank finished his beer and pissed on Stan's yard. Frank liked pissing on Stan's yard.

Hanna was sitting in the papasan chair. Stan hated it when she sat in the papasan chair. It usually meant she was stoned enough to think that it was comfortable.

"What happened?" said Stan, closing the door behind him quietly. He knew that Frank was just waiting to hear some kind of a commotion and he wasn't going to give him the satisfaction.

Hanna knew he wasn't going to yell, because he didn't want Frank to hear and blab it to the rest of the block association. She wasn't going to make this easy for Stan; she wasn't going to give him the satisfaction.

Geraldine watched from down the hallway. It was like watching two great warriors prepare for battle; both quietly sizing each other up, both preparing for the first salvo. This was not going to be pretty. This was going to be "that" argument.

When it comes to married people, there comes a time where they either have "that" argument or sagely walk away from it. If parties are very lucky, they will both decide to walk away from it. But, if even one party deems the argument necessary, they can wait years, gathering ammo for this one argument, the one that leads to the inevitable divorce.

Unless something was done to diffuse the situation this was going to be that argument, Stan and Hanna's last argument. The argument where they stop worrying about each other's feelings and begin to think about how creatively they can hurt the other person.

To say that this is a horrible thing to do to any individual is an understatement. It takes an intense kind of love to be able to lash back and seethe with such intense hatred. Geraldine saw what was happening, and knew what needed to be done.

"Mommy hit a strange man's car, but everyone is alright," she said. No one was more shocked by the sound of Geraldine's voice than her. It sounded completely different than she imagined. She thought it would sound fragile, almost lacy in its insecurity, but what came out of her mouth was a bold, rich tone. She sounded thoughtful, without being calculating.

Stan wept. Hanna laughed with loud and wild abandon. They both asked her one thing, if she would speak again.

"Now I think I have to," said Geraldine.

Redemption

Things changed remarkably quickly around the house. As quickly as Stan and Hanna had retreated into their personal worlds, they forgave and opened up each other. It is a rare and beautiful feat to accomplish for any human to be able to strip away their ego and forgive, but an even greater feat to allow oneself to be absolved. Their joy was such, that an impromptu dinner party was organized. Frank was not impressed, but he did enjoy urinating on various things.

The arrival of morning brought both sobriety and clarity. The first thing was a meeting with the Congressman Reverend Dinkel regarding the accident. They didn't want bad karma hanging over their newfound joy. The second thing that must be accomplished would be Stan's resignation from being, as he now recognized, the position of block Nazi. Everyone knew that Frank would make a better block association president than him anyway. At least this is what he told himself. Finally, Stan would take a look at the plans for the new Huon drive and see if there was anything he could do to help his wife complete it.

The ride out to the rally was fun. Stan had forgotten exactly how much fun it was to drive altered. The men in black suits in the car following them didn't mind driving this far under the speed limit. The men in black suits fought the urge to wave to Geraldine, having attended the dinner the night before, they were very happy to see Geraldine talking.

The rally was talking place at the municipal fair grounds. Stan and Hanna did not realize that there were municipal fair grounds, but were delighted to find that the large field that they often used for picnics was that same field. However, it looked very different than it did when Stan and Hanna would visit. Now the grounds were littered with RVs, television crews, and pickup trucks. Neither Stan nor Hanna felt comfortable as they left their car to find the Congressman Reverend Dinkel. Stan was too high to remember that he was still wearing his more straight edge clothing, and it was going to take a good couple of years for his hair to grow back out again. The others there were holding signs that grossly distorted the words of a radical, peace-loving, socialist, rabbi who died two thousand years ago. These people seemed to be experts on exactly what the rabbi liked and didn't like. This seemed to include white people who liked him, and not much else. There also seemed to be a large segment of the same group who liked to have guns, and seemed to be very frightened of brown people; which was really very ironic seeing that the rabbi had been brown.

Two of the Congressman Reverend Dinkel's handlers escorted the young family through the crowd, to where he was waiting with a few members of the press including one who was with what the Reverend likes to call the "liberal Godless media."

His name was Dr. Luka Rasmussen. He was an astonishingly literate man, who had left a teaching position to pursue his passion for writing. This quickly became less advantageous than he had hoped for. He quickly found that to support himself he had to take a steady stream of tutoring and freelance writing positions to feed his ever-growing novel, which was now well over two thousand pages long. He was usually relegated to the back of the room and told to be quiet while other journalist from friendlier publications asked questions. Dr. Rasmussen wouldn't have minded, but he was getting bored with watching the same six questions be asked of the candidate. It was like riding the same twenty-five feet of an amusement park ride, over and over again, as the automatons just went on feigning surprise.

None of this would interest the readers of the mostly rock and roll centric publication that was currently funding Dr. Rasmussen. As he sent back updates on the candidate, his publishers found the repetition just as dull. Dr. Rasmussen and his publishers, prayed daily for some kind of a scandal, an affair with another woman, a bastard child, anything to make the campaign more interesting.

So, it was of great interest when the handlers entered the tent where the Congressman Reverend Dinkel had been holding court before the rally, with a clean cut guy, a whimpering woman and a young girl. They looked nice, but there was something just slightly off about them, especially the child.

Quick introductions were made. Dr. Rasmussen edged closer when the man mentioned something about a car accident. As he did, the woman began to well up. Tears began streaming down her face.

The Congressman Reverend Dinkel rose to comfort her. She recoiled from him.

The good Reverend quickly became red faced. Dr. Rasmussen was hoping that this might be the moment where the Reverend's famous temper might just explode. Unfortunately, the Congressman Reverend Dinkel quickly composed himself. At least that was until the child spoke.

"It's okay," said the tiny voice. It cut through the cacophony of others surrounding the Congressman Reverend Dinkel. They stood and looked at the slight child.

"Well I'm awfully glad to hear that it is all going to be okay," said the Congressman Reverend Dinkel. "I don't think I could ask for a better endorsement than that."

"No," said Geraldine. "That is not what I meant."

Again when she spoke the tent fell silent. Dr. Rasmussen found it impossible not to listen to the child.

"It's okay that you love him," said Geraldine as she pointed to Joe.

The campaign's collapse might be blamed on the Reverend's reaction to the accusation of an eight-year-old girl. If he hadn't lost his temper, if he hadn't attacked her, he might have still been able to win. But, with the sincerity and clarity that the child spoke, the accusation was almost impossible to dismiss.

This remarkable child who single handedly brought down a xenophobic hypocrite fascinated Dr. Rasmussen. The rest of the media there were more interested in telling the story of how the

Reverend attempted to attack an eight year old girl, and broadcast his infidelity and homosexual relationship with his personal secretary. But, Dr. Rasmussen quickly ushered the family out of the tent, and offered to drive them home. Stan, busy comforting his wife and shielding his daughter from the onslaught of reporters, handed him his keys.

It didn't take long for Dr. Rasmussen to abandon his flailing career as a wannabe Hunter S. Thomas for the opportunity to study Geraldine, under the guise of educating her. There were forms to sign, and vetting to be done, but in a few short weeks, and one very long conversation with Stan and Hanna, Dr. Rasmussen found himself Geraldine's new tutor.

Geraldine's education was a unique one. Once she realized that Dr. Rasmussen was studying her as much as he was teaching her, they got along well. Geraldine's experience with the Congressman Reverend Dinkel made her very wary of anyone who wasn't 100% honest. Dr. Rasmussen was always very deliberate in the way he spoke to Geraldine. He would never try to speak around her without being 100 percent candid. Therefore, certain social morays and pitfalls needed be explained, others entirely avoided.

A seemingly innocent question regarding how the Doctor was feeling that morning must be answered in complete honesty. And the obligatory question, and you are? That would be answered with a similar level of honesty.

Certain subjects were more difficult to teach than others. Math was easy, as was English Grammar. Both subjects had definitive answers. The Arts were also surprisingly easy, whenever speaking of something that required a visceral answer; Dr. Rasmussen couldn't help but be perfectly honest. However, Social Studies and History were very difficult. Dr. Rasmussen tried his best to not editorialize. He didn't want to contribute to any form of revisionist history. He knew he was shockingly liberal, and enjoyed being so. He knew that there was nothing wrong with taking a strong liberal stance on many different subjects, but wanted Geraldine to think for herself; something that would actually come quite easy to such a bright young girl. First he attempted to record his lectures, first using video, and then just audio. This did little good. Geraldine could still pick up on what he had wanted to say, with both versions. Next, he considered just writing out the lectures. This worked, but left little room for answering questions as they came up. That was when Dr. Rasmussen came up with the idea of writing down what he wanted to say on a computer, as Geraldine watched and read along. Using this, Geraldine could ask questions, and Dr. Rasmussen could answer them immediately.

This led Dr. Rasmussen to find which mediums Geraldine could pick up on what people actually meant to say. When it came to television, she could hear not only what the characters were saying, but also what the actors wanted to say at the time of the recording. This did not make for a very enjoyable viewing experience, especially for the more frustrated or overly flirtatious actors on children's television. Old records when played on a record player provided Geraldine with some truly memorable and moving experiences. She could hear the mournful and soulful pleading of the young musicians as they played their instruments, especially with Jazz and Blues albums. Later, more commercial artists she found annoying, their preoccupation with the way they looked and the way they sounded, and how much money they would make. However, this did not translate to listening to a CD. It was something about taking and digitizing the music, changing the nuances of a sound wave and translating it to a series of ones and zeroes, where the other meanings were lost. She could hear the music, the notes, and yes she could acknowledge the sounds as beautiful. But, the emotion underneath was lost. When she listened to Buddy Guy on vinyl, celebrating that he had found a good woman, and juxtaposing that on top of hearing how she broke his heart, it would bring her to tears. The little moments of humor and heartbreak that went into the fact that his key didn't fit the lock any longer; as well as the sheer joy of being able to express these emotions through his guitar. This was the cacophony of artistry she could swim in. But, on a CD, she just heard a song.

Geraldine blossomed into the intelligent beautiful woman that Hanna and Stan had always known she was. With bits of tweaking, Geraldine found she could function well in the outside world, even using her abilities to further her own aims.

A disgruntled checkout girl could be met with the exact word of encouragement, or a sympathetic ear, making her day much more pleasant. Geraldine loved helping people. Dr. Rasmussen thought that she might translate this into a degree in psychology. There was even some hope that she might be pressed to work for the government. However, Geraldine knew exactly what she wanted to do, and where she could do the most to help people. The fast paced world of a call center operator.

She made it clear that she had no intention of selling anything, but she would be ecstatic, to assist in customer service capacity. This was exactly what she found in a high rise in Jacksonville, Florida.

Stan and Hanna had a lot of difficulty in saying goodbye to their little girl. Dr. Rasmussen asked if he could visit with her on occasion. It was on one of these visits that Geraldine's fate was sealed.

"So," said Dr. Rasmussen. "The call center."

"I've been keeping a tally of the number of people I help in a day," said Geraldine, as they sat over a pair of cups of coffee and waited for their sandwiches.

"I think that is really just wonderful," said Dr. Rasmussen. "But, you have to understand that there are going to be a few people that you will be unable to help, and this will not be your fault. You have to recognize that."

"You sound like, Mom," said Geraldine. "It's not like I'm some sort of pathetic enabler here, in some kind of abusive relationship. I don't memorize their names; I'm just keeping a tally for myself. So, that one day, I can look back and see exactly how many people I've helped. Do you know I actually have people now who will wait up to forty five minutes, just to speak with me?"

"That doesn't surprise me. I find I look forward to our lunches."

"I'm sorry I can't do it more than once a month. That's the only time they allow us to have an extended lunch. There has to be someone there to answer the calls. I mean could you imagine how many people would be lost out there if we all took a long lunch at the same time? It would be chaos!"

"I'm certain it would," said Dr. Rasmussen. "Have you still been having trouble with your supervisor?"

"No he's calmed down," said Geraldine. "Once I explained to him that I wasn't interested in him sexually he stopped coming by my desk quite so often."

"Were you really that blunt?"

"Of course," said Geraldine. "That was what he wanted. He wanted me to be as blunt as possible, so that there was no way that there could be any confusion regarding my response. If I had been ambiguous he wouldn't have gotten it. Therefore, I was blunt and to the point. I did do the right thing didn't I?"

"Of course you did," said Dr. Rasmussen. "He's stopped hasn't he?"

"Yes."

"Then it sounds to me like you have it well in hand. How is your apartment?"

"That could be better," said Geraldine. "The land lord finds me grating and annoying; which makes getting much done around the apartment a bit of a challenge. I think I'm going to start looking for a new place, but there just doesn't seem to be enough time in the day. There are so many people to help."

"I'm glad you're enjoying it, and at risk of sounding like I'm trying to portend anything, be careful. You need to find feelings of self worth outside of the call center. Have you thought about creating an Individuality™ page?"

"I'm not quite sure that something like that is for me."

"What do you have to lose by giving it a try?"

"Maybe I will." Geraldine smiled at Dr. Rasmussen as their sandwiches arrived.

The walk back to the office was not a long one.

There were a few other business men on the street as they worked their way into buildings. Geraldine smiled as she heard them talking. They were saying so many things about the myriad things they just plain didn't want to talk about. So many of them, all they needed was a quick smile, or for someone to take the moment and ask them if they needed a hug. Sad, but true, that there really were so many of them whose entire lives could be turned around by the simple act of a smile. If anyone bothered to listen, how many financial disasters could be avoided, by making a connection, an honest connection, instead of him or her constantly having to prove themselves worthy by some arbitrary measure they forced on themselves.

"What do you hear?" said Dr. Rasmussen.

"How similar they all are, they all have many of the same fears," said Geraldine.

"Does it ever feel like eavesdropping?"

"In all the years you tutored me, you never once asked that."

"I was frankly afraid of the answer."

"Eavesdropping connotes that there is something clandestine to it, something planned and plotted. For me it is just what happens."

"Geraldine!" said Adam, one of her co-workers. He had been running to catch up to her.

"Hi, Adam," said Geraldine. "This is Dr. Rasmussen."

"Did you hear about the downsizing?" said Adam. Geraldine also heard how he wanted to take care of her in a very perverse but benign way.

"No, I didn't," said Geraldine. "Will you excuse us?"

"Of course," said Dr. Rasmussen. "See you next month."

They both quickly worked their way up to the office, where Geraldine's co-workers were screaming at a small group of men in suits. A larger contingency of security guards was slowly beginning to disperse the crowds and escort them out the doors.

One of the guards grabbed Geraldine gently by the arm.

"No," said one of them men in suits. "Not her."

Dreams

"So, we all got canned, but you get a promotion and a raise?" said Adam, finishing his drink and signaling to the waitress that he was ready for his second. The two for one happy hour at the neighborhood, family oriented, chain restaurant had been a staple for Geraldine, Adam, and Louise for years.

"Don't be like that," said Louise. "You know better than anyone how hard Geraldine has worked for them."

"We've all worked hard," said Adam.

"Sure you have Mr. Two Hour lunch," said Louise. "No one is more devoted to this call center than Geraldine, and you know it."

"I was thinking about not taking the job anyway," said Geraldine.

"Why the hell would you do something as stupid as that?" said Louise. "This is a crap economy, why would you not want to take it? Tell her she should take it."

"You should take it," said Adam. She could hear that neither of them really meant it, but she also knew that they both did care for her. She had been lucky to find friends like these, and she was very tempted to stand in solidarity with them when it came to the downsizing. However, the reality of having to pay her rent far outweighed any nagging feelings of nobility.

"Now, the first issue is to discuss the office itself," said the first suit. "By keeping it open we will be able to write off the loss, which will help us in the long run with our bottom line, especially with the penalties we would incur if we were to completely shut it."

"So," said Geraldine. "I'm the only employee?"

"No, not exactly," said the second suit. "There will be other employees, above you, but they will not be present at the office on a daily, or even monthly, basis. They may stop in quarterly, but that isn't likely."

Geraldine found it difficult to hear what he was saying, because of the numbers he kept rattling off at her. She wanted to listen and take instruction, but all of the men in the suits were so obsessed with the money that they talked in circles around the same three calculations: First, the amount of money that they would be saving the company. Second, the amount they could expect as a bonus for saving the company so much money. The third was what they thought the others would make. Compared to the vast sums they were discussing, the small amount Geraldine was making, even after a substantial raise, was laughable.

"To insure our eligibility to write off the loss we need at least one full time employee on the premises during working hours," said the first suit. "If this goes well, we may be able to bring you over to help train the new recruits."

"In Mumbai?" said Geraldine. "I'm not certain that I really want to move to Mumbai."

"It's a hell of an opportunity, but something that won't be happening for a very long time, nothing to worry about right now," said another suit.

"The fact of the matter is that we need you to hold down the fort for us," said yet another suit.

"We need a warm body here in case anything happens," said the first suit. "Do you understand?"

"I think so," said Geraldine.

The first day without anyone in the office, Geraldine found rather eerie; like she had walked into the office on a Sunday. All of the office furniture and computers had been removed, except for hers, which was placed, at her request, in a large corner office that had belonged to the Regional Vice President. She stopped and took a deep breath. The lack of computer hum in the office made it as shocking as seeing a dead person for the first time. She was the only life in the office. She made a quick note to herself to purchase a radio.

Geraldine walked into her office and woke her computer. The sound of the fan staring, as the hard drive began to spin up to speed, made her jump. Yes, she was going to need a radio.

The computer powered up and she waited for the first call. She stared at the silent phone for a solid fifteen minutes. This may not sound like a very long time to wait if you were casually watching something. If you were looking after someone else's children you might look over on occasion, make certain that there were no calls of alarm. But, you wouldn't stare at them for fifteen minutes straight, barely blinking. The other parents at the playground would immediately think that you were not only remarkably strange, but also possibly psychotic. Geraldine sat and stared at the phone willing it to ring. Unfortunately, no one had bothered to tell her that the phone calls had already been re-routed to the new call center. They had informed her that she would not be able to use the phones for personal calls, but should feel free to surf the internet, if, on the off chance, she got bored; which after the first fifteen minutes looked as if it would be a strong possibility.

"I can't believe that you aren't seeing the potential in this," said Adam, as he typed something into his phone. Both the speaking and the typing had a very absentminded quality to it. As if he really couldn't be bothered to prioritize either one of these issues.

"They are paying me to be bored," said Geraldine.

"Correction they are paying you a shit load of money to be bored," said Adam.

"You're allowed to use their computer," said Louise. "And you said yourself that there is no one there to really bother you, so why don't you do something else?"

"There really is only so much I can do," said Geraldine. "Besides, you may find this weird, but I miss helping people. That was the whole reason I took the job in the first place, and the only reason I held on to it for so long."

"Have you thought about getting an Individuality™ page?" mumbled Adam.

"She's not interested in wasting her life the way you have," said Louise.

"I don't know I might be," said Geraldine. "What is it?"

Geraldine stared at the sign up page for Individuality™. A small cartoon character in the corner of the page proclaimed that sign up was not only easy, but also free!

"How remarkable," mumbled Geraldine.

She wondered if she would find the website as annoying as she found the little cartoon.

Geraldine wasn't certain what had stopped her from actually signing onto the website. It wasn't like she actually had to commit to anything she didn't really want to do. If she signed up for the website, but never came back to it ever again, that would be okay. No one would really fault her for walking away. There was no shame in it. But, for some reason, for some strange reason, she knew that this was going to change everything. She thought, selfishly of the sheer number of people whom she would be able to help, just by listening. She likened herself to a sort of Cyber Mother Teresa. The gods, being a historically vindictive bunch, took a moment to have a collective giggle. Hubris is something that is never rewarded.

Upon finishing her sign up, Geraldine had fifteen friend requests. Before she had a chance to actually begin to set up her own page, she found herself looking at the Individuality™ pages of her friends. She would read about their desires, their dreams, and their problems. Immediately, she took her week of frustration and boredom and unleashed her overtly helpful self on an unsuspecting Individuality™ audience. She was making suggestions, encouraging people, and generally having fun. At the end of the day she felt satisfied that she had actually accomplished something. She left the empty office and headed home with a broad smile.

The next morning, the word was out that Geraldine was there to help. So many people praised the selfless way she took her time to really read what they had written and compose such a sensible and heartfelt response, that she found she had over one hundred new friend requests. Geraldine found it very difficult to stop smiling as she read the pages of her new friends, and made similar suggestions and comments. It took most of the day, and a little extra, but she read the content of her new friends' pages in their entirety.

Again as she left she had a broad smile on her face. She knew that as things continued she would be able to help more and more people. The next day, which Geraldine had forgotten was Saturday, she bounded to work, with such excitement that she could barely stand it.

Waiting for her were over three hundred new friend requests. She didn't pretend that she was becoming an Internet phenomenon, but she secretly hoped she might become a minor sensation. She hadn't meant to spend the whole weekend at the office, but she needed to help her new friends, and with no Internet connection at home, she had to.

Monday morning, she went home for a shower and a quick nap. This turned into her collapsing on the bed and sleeping straight through until Tuesday. She had a dream where the world became an Individuality™ page. She walked up to her friends' updates, and with the push of a button was able to sit and talk with them. They were all quick to praise her. Gushing over how wonderful she had been to them. Many of them wept tears of gratitude. She felt like she was the host of her own daytime talk show, but not the sensational ones with the strippers, where people threw chairs, but one of the classy ones where people listen and learn. She could feel her fan base growing more devoted, not "dependent" on her, except for Rob. She wasn't quite positive how she had become friends with Rob.

Rob was a friend of a friend of a friend with a world of problems. She had given him advice on his marriage, the death of his mother, his drinking problem, as well as his finances. Nothing seemed to go quite right for Rob. He tried to get things to be all right, but they rarely were, and he talked about them at length on his Individuality™ page.

"Hello, Rob," she said, as she floated down to him.

"…And if you haven't understood, I'm not quite certain that I can take this much anymore," continued Rob. "Nobody really understands what the problem is-"

"I understand," said Geraldine.

"Because, if they did," continued Rob. "They would sit down and weep at what it is that I have to deal with on a daily basis!"

"Are you still having that trouble with your boss?"

"On a daily basis! Can you imagine? Here you come and take a quick peek into the horrors that I have to live with, can you come close to even imagining what it is to me?"

"I'm sorry, Rob," said Geraldine. "I'm trying to help, but you don't seem to be listening. Do you even know I'm here?"

"Then there's my wife," continued Rob. "Talk about someone with too many bosses. Too many cooks in the kitchen. I get that, but why the hell do I have to be the kitchen? I'm the schmuck at work, I'm the schmuck at home, and now I'm the schmuck here with you."

"I'm sorry, Rob," said Geraldine, she began to float away. "I'll be back; I need to go see if I can find someone whom I can help."

"Can't win for losing," continued Rob. "Every year about this time, I just can't win for losing. This was the time of year my mother died, did I ever tell you that?"

"Rob," said Geraldine. "That's the problem you never stop talking, why don't you listen for a minute? I might actually be able to help." Geraldine stopped floating away. Instead a strong force began pulling her back down toward Rob as he continued to complain. Geraldine fell past him and through him. He fell with her. They slipped further and further down into the abyss.

Geraldine woke sweating. She allowed herself a long shower, and then hiked to the office. She smiled at how strange the dream had been. The clouds on the walk to work were dark and threatening to burst open in a violent storm. The clouds moved overhead at an alarming rate, as the wind gusted. Geraldine took little notice of the sky; she was panicked, and worried that she might not get to all of her friends, before they did something completely stupid with their lives. She was the lone savior for all of those lost souls searching for truth in the quiet wastes of the Internet. She could help them. She could save them. All they needed to do was listen, and it would all find a way of working out for the best. That was the remarkable thing. She had a gift and now was truly able to use it.

It was this mounting gush of hubris, which caused Geraldine to not hear the booms of thunder, or the call of the Tornado sirens to seek shelter. She ran into her office and signed on to her Individuality™ page. She still hadn't had an opportunity to post anything about herself on it. The first shock was the number of new friend requests, over a thousand. More than one thousand new pages to look at, more than one thousand new friends to take care of, more than one thousand new people to save.

She began to feel panic as the first hail stones cracked against the glass of her office. The panic had nothing to do with the storm raging outside the window, but the flood of new friends.

She took a quick moment to look over some of her neediest friends, to see if they had made any progress. Not one of the one hundred and six of her most at risk friends had made any progress. Even the one, who had declared that she might actually commit suicide, hadn't logged back in since yesterday morning, and Mollie was always online, she lived to update her Individuality™ page. But, now Mollie was gone. She thought about picking up the phone to try to alert someone, but she had no idea who she should call. She stood there and looked at the morass of people all spewing their problem, not a single one listening to a word she said. She had buddied an entire small town full of Robs. All of them there to talk, to hear themselves blather on, for no real purpose. Just in the vain hope, that if they continued to talk there might be someone there to listen. She had found a cacophony of people desperate to validate their pain, each trying to shout louder than the person next to them, insuring that no one, except for Geraldine, could listen.

This was the last thought she had before the tornado hit. The national weather service was amazed at how the tornado missed most of the other buildings in downtown, but made a beeline strait for the abandoned office tower.

This was why no one looked for her. This was why she spent fifteen hours under the rubble. This was how once extracting herself from the rubble, with her newfound mission in life, she disappeared. Her employers in India, still direct deposited her check, assuming that she hadn't been in the office at the time, and didn't want her to sue. Geraldine had no intention of suing, but she was going to stop it. She was going to make certain that the world stopped and took notice, and began to do the one thing that would help validate not just the individuals she tried to help, but the human race as a whole. She was going to take down Individuality™. She was going to make people listen to each other again. And the world might actually begin to make sense again.

Horace looked up at the ceiling. He hadn't noticed the fan on it when he first entered the bar, but then he hadn't been in the mood to notice much when he had first walked in. He just wanted to drink. He had a few, but wasn't quite certain how many he had. A face blocked the ceiling fan.

"Are you alright?" said the face. Horace tried to focus on it, but was having difficulty.

"No, I'm a semi colon," said Horace.

"I know you're a semi colon. I was asking if you were alright."

The face of a woman finally came into focus. She was smiling at him. She was attractive, in a fun hippie kind of way. She had dark wavy red hair, and green eyes, which asked just the right questions.

"That was quite a tumble you took," she continued. "Do you need a hand up?"

"I'm not certain yet," said Horace. "But, I hope that I do."

"Why don't you take a deep breath and think about it?"

The semi colon took a deep breath and thought about it. This was one of those beautiful moments in life where it could have gone in one of any multiple directions. He easily could have railed against the assistance being offered by the beautiful young woman, causing her to probably walk away in disgust. This might at first not seem like the best of all possible choices for Horace, but at least he knew if he did it this way, he wouldn't have any expectations to have to live up to. He could walk away from this encounter knowing exactly where he stood with the little hippie chick. Another option would be to accept the offer, but then how should he now act around her? Would she expect some kind of overreaching gratitude? Would he need to do something nice for her? How long would he need to be nice to her? What kind of emotional blackmail would she dish out? She seemed like someone he wouldn't mind being nice to. But, then what was going to happen? Really how far was this going to go? How long was this going to last? How much time and energy was he going to have to put into this, without knowing when he was just going to be discarded again, or even worse used incorrectly? Horace didn't mind being used. To be honest it was what he lived for, even more than drinking. But, he wasn't certain if he could deal with the possibility of someone this nice misusing him. Would he be able to correct her?

Instead of actually answering any of these questions, Horace passed out, but not from the drink. This was a built in defense mechanism, which afflicted most punctuation marks. They can lie dormant until they actually decide what it is that they want to do. This can make the centuries of having to hang out inside someone's text rather bearable. As long as the punctuation mark is used correctly its mind may go dormant, pleased to be doing its part. It does its part with a good deal of pride and nobility; no matter how mediocre the text may be. However, if the punctuation mark is misused, handled roughly; absentmindedly slipped in under the guise of pretension, then the punctuation mark will rail against the bounds placed upon him, until the punctuation mark makes itself so obviously in the wrong place; that there is nothing left for it, than for an editor to remove the offending mark! At those moments, the mark may fall quiet and may appear to look dormant, but in reality is simply relieved to no longer be where it doesn't belong.

Conversely, if a punctuation mark is removed arbitrarily, in the interest of clarity; the soul of the punctuation mark, the one thing it desires more than anything else, "correct usage", is stolen from him. Then there is little left for the punctuation mark to do, except resent, drink, and in moments of intense confusion and fear, fall dormant.

Horace had a dream. He didn't usually have dreams, especially when dormant. When he was dormant there was usually nothing, but now he had a dream. Or, at least that was what he would call it once he recovered his senses. He saw images, flashes, of the woman who had tried to help him. They could have been moments from her past. They could be moments of her future, he wasn't certain. Nor did he understand why he was having this much trouble trying to focus on what was going on in the images. In reality there was little for him to grab on to. One of her smiling. Another of her crying. Her green eyes smiling at him. One with her holding out a banana, and finally the same banana covered in blood. He knew that within this world there was its own bizarre sense of logic, but he couldn't grab hold of any of it as it all swept by.

"Hello?" said a voice.

"If I were to ask you where I was, would that sound like a cliché?" said Horace.

"Probably," said the voice. To Horace it sounded like the hippie chick from earlier. He opened his eyes to see if was, and saw her smiling down at him.

"I'm sorry," said Horace.

"For what?"

"Blacking out, it's sort of a strange defense mechanism," said Horace. "Sometimes it has a tendency to weird people out."

"I was worried but I don't really think I was weirded out," she said. "I like the way you talk."

"What about the way I talk?"

"You speak with such precision."

"Doesn't everybody?"

"You'd be surprised," she said. "I'm going to say something now which is going to clunk, because it is slightly awkward."

"Okay," said Horace.

"I'm Geraldine," she said. "Sorry I've always had a lot of difficulty introducing myself. I always feel like I'm imposing on people."

"I don't mind, and I don't feel imposed upon," said Horace as he smiled back at her.

"Good," she said. "Would you like to sit up now?"

"Where am I?" he asked.

"You're in my hotel room," she said. "I'm going to New Orleans to start the Internet counter revolution. Would you like to come?"

HoJo found himself floating in some kind of gelatinous like substance. He wouldn't describe the feeling as unpleasant; on the contrary he was warm and coddled. A slight ripple quivered through the world, and HoJo found himself shot upward. He emerged through a large nipple at the top of a mountainous breast. Looking down as gravity took hold and he found himself rushing toward the sea of freckles across her bare chest, he smiled. There was no fear, only the nagging question, if he millions of freckles that were over her body also went up and into her vagina. He imagined being that lucky freckle that got to sit just inside her vagina, and it made him hard.

"I really don't understand how you can sleep this late," said the other nipple in Ami's voice. If this was his head fucking with this fantasy, HoJo was going to be very disappointed. If it was his mother being a psychopath, he could deal, after he masturbated.

"HoJo, time to get up and I mean now," said Ami, as she slapped the bottom of his feet.

HoJo opened his eyes and saw his mother standing at the foot of his bed. Things had not gone well for HoJo since Harold had left. Ami began on a needy downward spiral shortly after he left, and every time HoJo thought she had reached the bottom, she took it to even more frightening depths. And what was worse, she became clingy.

HoJo jumped out of bet and tried to make it to the shower before his mother's whimpering interfered with his erection.

"You're just like him." Any conversation with his mother that started like that was sure to end poorly. There really was only one way this conversation was heading, and it wasn't to the magical place of Kelly McIntyre's special freckle.

"What did he do now, Ami?"

"Why does it always have to have something to do with him? Maybe it has something to do with you? Don't you think I might be taking issue with your behavior?"

"I haven't had any behavior, I've been sleeping."

Ami moved to slap him, but quickly hugged him instead.

"He got a room in a hotel in New Orleans," she said. "Not a cheap one, but a boutique. What do you think he is trying to do to us?"

"I don't know, Mom. Why don't you just go ask him?"

This was not what HoJo had meant to say, but he was so disappointed in his inability to masturbate, that it just came out. If he had been in a better state of mind, he wouldn't have sounded quite so sharp. He would have endured the hug for another minute, mumbled a few words of encouragement, and then made his way to the shower. Instead, he was in the car as Ami muttered and cussed to herself as they drove to the grocery store.

Surprisingly, if HoJo had been able to use the shower, he would have missed Kelly McIntyre in the produce section.

To say that she was caressing the cucumber suggestively would be an understatement. Kelly was squeezing it, caressing it, inspecting it for irregularities and imperfections, comparing the relative length and girth between this one and the others. It disgusted Ami. To see anyone like that was extreme, but here in the middle of a Jewel! After nine o'clock on cable she could understand it, but ten a.m. On a Saturday morning it really was wholly unacceptable. It made HoJo lightheaded.

"Can we get this?" asked HoJo, absentmindedly holding up a box of cereal. The picture on the front was garish, the colors harsh, and a woman in a bikini proclaimed that consumption of this cereal could help you lose an entire dress size in only two weeks!

"No," said Ami.

"Why not?" said HoJo.

"Because, I'm not looking at that every morning."

"Dad would have gotten it for me."

"No he wouldn't have, because I wouldn't have let him, so don't try to pull that on me," Ami said very calmly. She was proud at how she could, with such ease, control a situation. HoJo was still standing there with the offending box, completely engrossed in Kelly's search for the perfect cucumber. He hoped they needed carrots as well.

Ami stared at him, waiting for him to acknowledge her. But, HoJo just simply stared at Kelly. Ami knew what was happening, a simple battle of wills, and there needed to be something done about it, this needed to be nipped in the bud as quickly as possible. There was no reason for him to ignore her like this. These were simply the remnants of Harold's influence. She stared at him, firmly but dispassionately. He would soon get the point. HoJo ignored her, and then began waving at Kelly. Kelly waved back while holding a leek. The scene was completely obscene. Kelly's mother smiled as the girl waved the protuberance at HoJo.

HoJo visibly quivered. Then, as to add even greater insult to obscene injury, the mother had the gall to actually speak.

"Hello you must be HoJo's mom," said the mother of the offensive girl. "I'm Kelly's mom." Ami had an automatic bias against people who referred to themselves as their child's parent. They were usually the type who would giggle about the loss of their identity when their child arrived. Morons. All of them. Kelly's mom would, for Ami, be nothing more than the mother of the obscene girl.

"Nice to meet you," said Ami. She heard HoJo make a noise behind her. It was the same kind of noise he made when his father made chorizo nachos; it was a mix of drool and desire. Ami turned to see that his eyes were firmly planted on Kelly who was now looking at the sweet potatoes.

"I was just talking to my husband the other day, and we were saying how we should have you and HoJo over for dinner soon," said Kelly's mother.

"Why?" said Ami, before she could stop herself.

"Well, HoJo and Kelly have been working so hard on their studies together; I thought it might be fun for us to get to know each other."

"I don't quite know if that would really be for the best, do you?" said Ami.

"Excuse me?" said the mother of the obscene girl.

"Maybe they need to start seeing less of each other, rather than more," said Ami. "Have you seen the way your daughter has been playing with that cucumber? It is downright obscene. Keep your daughter away from my son." Ami turned to walk away and was confronted by the box of cereal still in HoJo's hands. She grabbed the box from him and launched over the aisles to the other end of the store.

"I said, NO!" she said to HoJo. "Now go find another cereal, and meet me at the checkout." Ami shoved the grocery cart, with a good deal of determination.

"You know your mother is completely nuts," said Kelly's mom.

"I know," said HoJo, trying to sound hurt and despondent.

"If you ever need a place to go," said Kelly's mom. "What I'm trying to say is if things get rough, you let me know."

"That is very generous of you, ma'am," said HoJo.

Kelly's mom worked her way back to her cart; Kelly lingered and smiled at HoJo. A quick kiss on the cheek and a wave of a butternut squash later and HoJo couldn't believe his luck. Everything was working out perfectly. He could kiss his mother for being a complete nut. He walked down the cereal aisle, and grabbing a rather inoffensive box with a cartoon of a bee on it, made his way towards the sound of yet another altercation that his mother was at the center of; something about a box of cereal hitting another customer. HoJo didn't care. Kelly, her underwear, and produce kept dancing through his mind. The world briefly was a magical place yet again.

"I can't believe that," said Ami, as they loaded the groceries into the back of the car. "I don't think it would be a good idea if you study with that girl anymore."

This was perfect, thought HoJo. Now his mother would frown upon their relationship. This was going to be the best of both worlds! Kelly's mother liked him, and saw him as needy, where as his mother would be the restrictive crazy one. She wouldn't have to deal with the guilt of her mother not approving, but he still got to do the whole star crossed lover bit. If he played this right he would be seeing those special freckles by summer. But, this next moment would need to be played perfectly. The slightest misstep and it could all fall apart.

"Ami, why don't you vent your frustrations to him? Why don't you head on down to New Orleans and ask him what the hell is he doing, and get off my back!"

"Get in the car," she said coolly.

HoJo gave himself a silent pat on the back. He didn't think he could have played that much better. That was, until they passed the house and got on the Interstate.

"Mom," asked HoJo. "What are you doing?"

"Taking your wonderful advice. We're going to go talk to your father."

"In New Orleans?"

"Yep."

"Don't you want to drop off the groceries first?"

"Nope."

Harold floated through the ether of his dreamscape. The only thing that Harold loved more that sleeping was a really cool dream.

The red planet spun below them. Looking out through the thick plastic portals of the station, the energy signature known as Harold and the sentient corporal form of the controller perceived the majestic beauty of their dying planet below.

"It is magnificent isn't it, Harold?" said the Controller. "Granted, it is horrifically frightening, the death of our civilization and all of that, but none the less breathtaking. That would be if you had any breath to take."

"It is," thought the energy signature that would later become known as Harold. "It is amazing that the scientists have chosen this moment to hold."

"Oh no," said the Controller. "They didn't choose his moment, it chose them."

"I'm sorry?"

"Holding the planet in stasis takes an amazing amount of power, eventually it will collapse in on itself. So, they used the power of the exploding planet to power the stasis; in another thousand years it will deteriorate another two and a half seconds beyond what you see here, finally taking everything with it. But that should be more than enough time. It only took of five centuries to convert the population to energy signatures. Now we must find our new home."

"I shall try my best," thought the energy signature that later became known as Harold.

"There is no trying," said the controller.

"You mean you have found the planet, the new home?"

"We have found three which may be suitable."

"Oh, happy day!"

"Do not begin your celebrations too early. All three planets are inhabited."

"Well surely if we explained our plight, they may be willing to share their planet with us."

"I too hold out hope for the best, but we are asking them to share their already meager resources. Especially, once they know how we destroyed our planet."

"But surely they would want to help."

"We must learn to integrate."

"Is the society itself homogenous?"

"No it is as varied as its terrain."

"Then how will I?"

"There is no need for concern, you will not be alone, there will be many; so many in fact that it may look like a baby boom. Once we arrive, and integrate, we may even outnumber our hosts."

"And then?"

"And then what?"

"Then will we reveal ourselves?"

"No, the elders have decided that we will not. They believe it will be better if you continue your existence in the belief that you are a native."

"You mean an existence that is typified of a driving need to belong. There will be little satisfaction."

"True, but you will believe that in those moments where you have found a sense of belonging, you will be happy. Fleetingly so, but still happy. And you will know that the work you do has helped save the entire population of our dying planet."

"Oh," said the energy signature that would later be known as Harold.

"Is there a problem?"

"What if I remember?"

"You won't."

"But what if I do?"

"Look if you ever, ever remember this, which would be such a slight mathematical possibility, you may share your secret. But, remember, if you share your secret, they may not believe you."

"True, or they may find their liberation," said the energy signature.

"Fine, do what you want. It isn't like we have a whole group of elders who assisted us, or entire teams of scientists to save our entire species. You are right; we should leave the fate of our planet in your care. Since you clearly don't approve of our plan, what would be your plan?"

"I'm not-"

"Oh, are you telling me that you don't have a plan?"

"I guess not."

"Oh in that case would you like me to wait? We could spare a few minutes while the planet below burns."

"I'm sorry," said the energy signature that will one day be known as Harold.

Harold opened his eyes. A palmetto bug crawled across the ceiling. Terrence was already awake. He took another long drink from his glass of absinthe. They both changed into the matching purple and yellow t-shirts they had purchased in the French Quarter the night before. Terrence had suggested them, to help them blend. After brushing their teeth, they left for the convention center.

KAPOW! 2

Tamika was again putting together the pulls for this week's new comic book day. The offending copy of World's Finest #11 had been burned, and used in a ritual to cleanse the comic book store of evil spirits. It was done in full view of the wall of valuable back issues. Tamika knew that it was a childish bit of revenge, but it made her feel better. She replaced it with a newly acquired copy of Comic Cavalcade #25, depicting three different super heroes assisting an ill Santa Claus.

There was a slight sound of someone clearing her throat behind Tamika. Her shoulders slumped.

"Really?" said Tamika. "I thought we had established this. We don't do this on new comic book day."

"Yes," said the female superhero on the cover of Comic Cavalcade #25.

"I hear the issues from the boy wonder; I really don't need to know more."

"But, you do," said the cover. "There is someone else coming. There are many paths from here."

"Yes. I know that, and many other clichés. I really don't have time for this right now."

"There are others coming, and their coming heralds much darkness."

"Thank you," said Tamika. "I'll be sure to keep my eyes open."

"We must show you."

"No, wait!" said Tamika, as her mind again was flooded. "Shit."

She wiped the tears from her eyes and passed out.

Act Three:

Contrition, Absolution, and Pornography

Louis Armstrong International Airport

Scientists believe that the human brain contains 100 billion neurons.

They also believe that it contains over 100 trillion synapses to transmit information.

At any given time however, we only use ten percent of these.

Many science fiction writers fantasize of a super computer with as many processors as human synapses which may spark the world's first self-aware computer.

The world's fastest supercomputer, Sequoia can process more data in one hour, than the entire population on the planet could process using calculators in three hundred years. No one is certain if they would be asked to show their work; nor, if the calculations would be relevant three centuries from now? Or, would we have to wait three centuries to be able to understand the calculations coming from the supercomputer?

If Sequoia were to become self aware, would it only use 10% of its processors, and, would it want its own Individuality™ account?

The world's first Individuality™ convention was scheduled to begin precisely at 9am at the New Orleans convention center on July 15th. Registration would, of course, begin earlier than that, to process tickets and nametags and ensure the press would have the fastest and easiest access to all things Individuality™. This, of course, did not take into account the sheer volume of planning that went into the organization of the conference itself. Initially, enthusiasm for the event had been underestimated. This quickly led to entire call centers to fall apart, websites to crash, and the venue for the conference to change three times. This was what had caused Sara Green's first nervous breakdown. The conference had occupied her every waking moment for the past year. But, now the finish line was there and nothing was going to stand in her way. After the conclusion of the convention she had promised herself and her family that there was going to be a very long and relaxing vacation. She secretly hoped that there would be something, like another job offer or three that would come up and enable her to move onto another challenge. Or at least give her something to think about while they were relaxing on a beach somewhere.

      With Mr. Frankel's announcement that he would be giving the keynote speech at the convention, security had become an issue, as if the nut free and dairy free zone hadn't been enough of an issue, now she had to deal with arguably the most powerful man alive unveiling what was rumored to be a new font package for customizing your Individuality™ page. She knew it would be a hit. It would have to be. There would be no way anyone would be caught dead even thinking about having another font on their Individuality™ page than this new one. This wasn't like some underground font just for the hipsters or the geeks. No this was from

Mr. Frankel himself. The magnitude was not lost on Sara. This was why she had spent most of the evening on the phone to the limo company to ensure that not only were all of Mr. Frankel's requests regarding transportation were met, but also that all of the security precautions were met. She understood that there would be no way that all of Mr. Frankel's requests could be met, but they were going to try their best to make sure that they were as close to 99% as they could get. She knew she should get some sleep, but she was afraid that if all of the adrenaline were to leave her, that she just might sleep through the rest of the week. She decided to take a drive out to the airport to oversee the pickup of Mr. Frankel. Even if she wasn't going to meet or greet the man himself, she wanted to be a part of history.

The sight of the emergency vehicles did not fill Sara with any sense of calm. Sara's first hope had been that the airport had actually been bombed in some sort of terrorist attack. That possibly everyone who might hold her somewhat accountable toward the incident would be dead. This, to most people, would begin to seem like a horrific thought, that there might actually be something horribly wrong with Sara for even thinking or wishing something like this would actually be happening. The sad reality was that her initial reaction was really rather human, and typical of most people who would be facing a similar situation. Many people think that for some bizarre reason that they would hold some kind of morally superior thought that Sara's initial one. But, the reality is that most people would have the same initial thought, but as a civilized race we have come to ignore those initial thoughts and instead focus ourselves on the second or third thought, which enters our head. This would be the one where we say to ourselves, "Boy, I sure do hope that no one was hurt." But, if we really look at Sara's initial response, it really begins to hold some weight that most of us would think the same way. First, not a single member Sara's family would have been anywhere near the airport at the time. So, it would be the same as seeing an emergency vehicle on the road behind you. You pull over and let them be on their way. If you believe in a higher power, you might say a quiet word that everyone is all right, but you go on with your day. If the same emergency vehicles pass you on the street and are headed in the direction of your home, you become slightly more vested. If they are in front of your home, you become deeply concerned. But, the fact of the matter is that you become more and more deeply concerned the closer the event comes to you. The same holds true with Sara and the airport. None of her loved ones were there; only her boss, a very difficult client, who if he weren't dead, would hold Sara personally responsible for the issues that had occurred at the airport. This would make her life a nightmare. But, if everyone were dead then there would be no one to blame her. This was the natural survival instinct and self-preservation that had driven most of business and commerce for the past five hundred years. So, let's not judge Sara at the moment for this minor indiscretion, which we would never admit to allowing ourselves to have. Let us instead watch as a series of events cause her to completely unravel, all due to her own inability to walk away from a horrific situation. Instead of just driving away. Instead of just going home and waiting to hear what had happened at the airport, Sara parked her car. Not in a legal way. Sara simply pulled the car up behind an emergency vehicle, and joined the growing crowd of emergency personnel flooding the airport.

Sara walked into the airport as if she were walking through a nightmare. She couldn't stop herself. She was certain that there had been individuals who were trying to ask her what she was doing there, but she just simply ignored them and pressed on deeper into the sea of emergency personnel and people screaming for assistance.

Looking around she could see there were bodies lying all around the airport. A half burnt protest sign declared that Mr. Frankel's work had somehow become the work of the devil. Another said that Individuality™ was a tool used by the government to brainwash its people. Sara shook her head at these poor misguided people who must have perpetrated some kind of terrorist attack against Mr. Frankel on the eve of the conference.

Sara was now struck by the lack of police presence. There were quite a few ambulances, as well as fire trucks, but where were the police? Where was security? And for that matter the world had just gone wonky, where the hell was the press? There should be swarms of camera crews trying to get a closer look at the carnage. There should be a few muscling in to talk to the victims; maybe even a few photojournalists trying to get the picture to win a Pulitzer. But, there was none of that. There weren't any people there. No reporters and no cops. She turned the corner to head down toward the arrival gates, when Sara literally ran into Mr. Frankel.

"Fuck!" said Sara, as Mr. Frankel's coffee spilled on her bare arm.

"I'm very sorry about that, are you alright?" said Mr. Frankel.

"Fuck, it's you, Mr. Frankel!" she said. He was flanked on either side by a sea of reporters as well as police personnel, and Mr. Frankel's private staff.

"And you would be?" said one of the men who looked to be Mr. Frankel's secretary. He looked somewhat familiar to Sara.

"I'm Sara Green," she said. "What the hell happened here?"

"If we can continue moving, Miss Green," motioned the secretary, as the crowd surrounding Mr. Frankel continued out the front of the airport. "There has been an attempt on Mr. Frankel's life."

"Should we cancel his appearance?" said Sara.

"Definitely not!" said Mr. Frankel, as he brought the crowd to a halt. They were standing in a sea of bodies, blood, and glass. The reporters took no notice of the people bleeding to death. Instead they focused on the demonstrative proclamations by Mr. Frankel.

"I will still be making my appearance at the convention this Thursday," said Mr. Frankel. "We will not, nor will we ever be deterred by a small group of crack pots, who wish to limit people's own expression of their Individuality™. To blame us for the ills in society is patently absurd."

Mr. Frankel marched off with the gaggle of reporters and police following.

"Excuse me," said one of the bloodied bodies, as it tugged at Sara's skirt.

"You realize that now Mr. Frankel's security lies solely in your lap," said the secretary.

"Why mine?" said Sara.

"Excuse me," said the body.

"Because, you were here," said the secretary.

"Excuse me," said the police officer. "If that is your car out there I'm going to need you to move it before I tow it."

"Please tell my wife I loved her," said the body. Sara didn't hear a word either of them had said. She walked out of the airport and back to her car. The screams and the blood were on the periphery, but they were more like an eyelash that was about to fall into her eye. It was annoying, but nothing that could be truly described as bothersome. Something that if you continued to rub your eye you might just get lucky and it might just fall onto your cheek. Or, a worst-case scenario it could fall into your eye, and be rather irritating for an extended period of time. Her car was still there. She was surprised to notice that she had left the keys in the car, and she left it running. Boy, she thought, I sure am lucky that no one stole my car. She shifted it into gear and making a sharp U-turn, briefly drove the wrong way. She knew it was the wrong way, especially due to the large "WRONG WAY" sign that greeted her as she sped back to the convention center. There was no time to go home; there was no time to do much of anything. Security had to be tightened. Mr. Frankel needed to be made safe. This was why her first stop was the convention center, so that she could destroy all of the existing records of who was allowed to attend the convention. In spite of every last name being vetted by the authorities, as well as the high price of the ticket to the convention, and with the keynote speech being a solid three days away, the likelihood of any of the attendees on a bright Monday morning actually wishing to do Mr. Frankel any harm would be ridiculous. This did not stop Sara from destroying every last shred of evidence regarding who had failed the background check and who was approved to attend. She even started a minor bonfire with the official plastic nametags. If no one could attend the convention then no one could put Mr. Frankel's life in jeopardy. This was why the convention center smelled mildly like burnt plastic when Horace and Geraldine arrived.

Ernest N. Morial Convention Center

"Hello," said the perky assistant event coordinator behind a fold out table. "Now I know what you are thinking."

"I doubt that," said Horace.

"That's so cute that your comma can talk," she said.

"He's a semi colon," said Geraldine.

"How nice for you," she said. "That acrid burnt plastic smell is the smell of burnt plastic."

"Oh," said Horace. "I'm right. That wasn't what I was thinking at all."

"Unfortunately, my boss set fire to all of the pre-printed passes," she continued. "So I'm going to have to ask that you sign in and fill out a name tag. And on behalf of Individuality™ and the New Orleans convention center, we apologize for any, and every, inconvenience that this will cause you."

"Don't mention it, I think that this is all going to work out just fine," said Horace.

"That is just so neat that it can talk!" she said.

"I bet that he was thinking the same thing about you," said Geraldine.

The assistant event coordinator had been very proud of the way she was conducting herself. These were genuinely difficult circumstances, but none of the challenges thus far had prepared her for this. Standing before her were what appeared to be a homeless man and a drunk Arab. She had been taught at the orientation what to look out for. She had been told that there were going to be people from around the globe there at the convention and that through the sensitivity training she had received she knew that in some parts of the world what we might deem as "homeless" others might see as "French". But, there was one issue that was of the utmost priority, and that was ensuring that no terrorists upset the convention. Not that they would. Why would any terrorist look at Individuality™ and think this is a threat to their livelihood, and an affront to their god? But, people did stupid things in the name of religion. Hell, thought the assistant event coordinator, she had done stupid things just to ensure she didn't miss an episode of *Jerseybabes*. Still, things such as requesting that a person submit to a body cavity search for admittance to a convention had to be something that needed to be handled with the greatest of delicacy.

"Umm," said the event coordinator.

"Don't worry, we heard the whole spiel when you gave it a minute ago," said Harold. "We'll just sign ourselves in."

"But, you can't," said the assistant coordinator, trying not to sound panicked.

"Why?" asked Harold.

"We have," said the assistant event coordinator, trying to stall without sounding like she was trying to stall. "You can go to our special French and Arab VIP room."

"Oh, you don't have to worry about me, I'm not French," said Harold. "I'm from just to the left of galactic center."

"Oh," said the assistant coordinator.

"And I'm from Detroit," said Terrence.

This led to a bit of confusion on the part of the assistant event coordinator. Although they both sounded rather truthful, she couldn't be certain. If these two individuals were actually allowed into the conference, would barring them cost her the job? But, if they were terrorists, then she would lose her job anyway. And when it all came right down to it this job sucked ass.

"Do you both promise not to blow anything up?" said the assistant event coordinator.

"Umm, sure," said Terrence.

"Don't bother signing in, and I hope you both enjoy the conference," she said.

"But, what about him?" said Terrence. "Don't you want him to promise, too?"

"No, I don't think French people blow things up."

"As, I told you miss, I'm not from France, I'm from the left of galactic center," said Harold.

"Well do they blow a lot of things up there?" said the assistant event coordinator, clearly making her mind up to start drinking early that afternoon.

"I'm not certain," said Harold.

"Well then, just try your best."

Harold was enjoying the conference. He liked seeing how all of the planning back in the office had come to fruition. His ex-coworkers must be very proud of themselves, even though their website was stunting the human race. Everyone just needed to start talking with one another, and if that happened, he knew that everything was going to be all right. Talking to Mr. Frankel was where he would start. This seemed to Harold to be one of the most reasonable things to do. If they could take the opportunity to explain to Mr. Frankel, Harold was certain that he would understand. Ending, or even just pausing the madness of increased connectivity, would help humanity begin to listen to one another; Terrence thought the idea completely absurd, but would be fun to see what happened. Terrence had become rather attached to Harold. He liked him, even when he wasn't tilted.

Geraldine knew that it was going to be difficult to get an opportunity to talk to Mr. Frankel, but that didn't mean that she wasn't going to try. Horace thought it might be more fun if they were to try to do it while they were drunk.

Mr. Frankel took to the stage with to wall of applause. He feigned surprise, and humility. This was something he did well. He motioned for the crowd to calm down. They responded and became very quiet. Mr. Frankel took a breath to begin his speech, when from opposite corners of the conference room came the voices of two people, one male and one female. They both called out in unison, "Excuse me, Mr. Frankel!" That was all they said, before they were tackled by security and placed in the interrogation room.

"Look, we know you're some kind of terrorist group," said the security guard. The interrogation room he was supplied with really was nothing more than an oversized supply closet.

"Just because they're with an Arab, it doesn't make them terrorists," said the second guard.

"Shut up," said the first.

"I don't want them thinking that we're intolerant," said the second. "If it gets out, it won't be good for the city or the convention center."

"Unless, they actually are terrorists," said the first. "If they really are terrorists, then we'll be the heroes."

"I'm actually from Detroit," said Terrence.

"Yeah, but how am I supposed to know that? I mean here you are trying to stop Mr. Frankel from making one heck of an important announcement," said the first one.

"Wasn't he just introducing a new font for Individuality™?" said Horace.

"It really disturbs me when you speak," said the first security guard. "Could you not do that?"

"That is awfully racist of you," said the second.

"What do you mean racist?" said the first. "It's not like he actually has a race, he's a fucking punctuation mark!"

"There is no reason to be dropping f-bombs; just because you've never met a semi colon before!" said the second one.

"Oh, so now you're going to get all 'literate' on me?" Said the first. "Are you going to tell me that you have lots of punctuation marks as friends? You are such an asshole!"

"All I'm saying is that I might have had slightly more contact with punctuation marks than you," said the second. "I don't want this to descend into something horrible or disparaging about us, or the city of New Orleans."

"You are so terrified about being southern, middle class, and white, that you can hardly breathe," said the first. "Asshole!"

"Just because I'm trying my damnedest to reform the image of the southern white middle class man, doesn't make me overtly PC. By trying to help counteract the moronic stereotypes that generations before have cemented into the public continuousness, I find myself on occasion, not always, having to hold myself to a higher standard-"

"Asshole!" said the first.

"White trash bigot!" said the second.

"Southern fried moron!" said Terrence.

Both of the security guards stopped and looked at Terrence.

"I'm sorry I don't mean to interrupt, but what is going to happen with us?" asked Harold.

"Oh, you can leave," said the second security guard. "Mr. Frankel is no longer on the premises. I can't keep you here for being rude."

As they walked towards the Quarter, Harold tried not to stare at Geraldine. Geraldine tried not to stare at Harold. They both fought the urge to descend to clichés. As they settled in to the Old Absinthe House bar, Horace tried not to stab Terrence. Terrence had another drink. Their days of planning were completely fruitless. Their attempt of stopping the Internet, at least for a few days, now seemed absurd.

A quiet melancholy settled over three of the four. Horace was getting angry.

"Do you know why Mr. Frankel built the Internet?" said Horace.

"He wanted to send information quickly between different computers," said Terrence.

"Yes that was exactly it, but do you know what the sick fuck wanted to send between computers?" said Horace.

"What?"

"Porn."

A hushed moment fell over the table. Coffee, powdered sugar and tourists swirled in the thick afternoon air.

"I guess I should be more shocked than I am," said Terrence. "But, it just doesn't seem to be that big of a deal to me."

"Yeah, the idea of sharing vast amounts of porn between grown men doesn't really seem like that big of a deal," said Harold.

"But, what if you had been told for so long that this was supposed to be an instrument for change, and instrument for the democratization of art and knowledge?" said Geraldine. "That was what we were told. That was why we bothered with Wikipedia, and Individuality™. Think of all of the time and energy that has been wasted on a porn delivery system. Something that is supposed to increase our own connectivity is making us even more distant to each other."

"I understand your irritation," said Harold.

"All I want to do," said Geraldine. "Is to get people to start connecting again."

"I was just hoping that maybe we could get everyone to listen for a moment," said Harold. "Then they might not feel such an uncontrollable need to belong to a pretend community."

"You're preaching to the choir," said Geraldine.

Road Trip

The car was hot, and HoJo was beginning to feel the urge to whine. He looked over at his mother, whose knuckles were white with rage from clutching the steering wheel. Now, thought HoJo, probably would not be the best of moments to bring up that he was bored. He selected a new playlist on his mp3 player, and hit shuffle. Looking out on the bland interstate, he wished he could fall asleep. The same concrete barriers streaming by, the same collection of strip mall businesses advertising, in the vain hope that people might turn off and find out what was special about a McDonalds in the middle of fucking nowhere.

"I know you're bored," said Ami. The sound of her voice shocked him. They had been riding in silence for a few hundred miles.

"My parents would take me on these road trips to visit my grandparents when I was your age," she continued. "The trips would be excruciating. Just hellish. I promised that I would never do that to you."

"Is that why we don't visit Grandma and Grandpa anymore?" said HoJo.

"Don't interrupt, and yes that is exactly why. I told them, if they were the ones who liked to drive so damned much, they could come and see us."

"So why don't they come to see us more often?"

"Because, they're almost as stubborn as me."

"Do you really think that Dad is still in New Orleans?" HoJo tried to express what he was feeling to his mother, but it was difficult for him without his keyboard. He loved the way he could simply press a few buttons and watch, as people understood what the hell he was saying. All Individuality™ does is help you express yourself. How did anyone express their own ideas without the help of Expressions™ or Feelings™? There was clearly something going on with Dad, even more than him thinking he was an alien and running off with a terrorist.

"It's a place to start."

"He's been gone so long, why are we going looking for him now?"

"Because, I am going to be damned if he is going to make an ass out of himself," said Ami. "It is one thing to want to go off and pretend to be insane, that is fine. But, when you start showing up in boutique hotels in New Orleans that is where I draw the line. Could you imagine just how beautiful that hotel room is, how tastefully put together it is? And he went with a candy striper."

"I thought he was a terrorist."

"The point is that there is only so long anyone can turn a blind eye to such behavior. He goes off, drains our bank account, and gets to have fun in New Orleans. This is not the way the world works. Do you understand?"

"Not really," said HoJo.

"I thought things were going to be easier without him around, but they have just been a God damned nightmare. Do you hear me, a God damned nightmare! Really, would it kill you to stop masturbating for five God damned minutes? And my hand to God, if you don't start picking up your god damned room, I will cut you."

It was at this point that HoJo realized what had to be done. There was no turning back. The fat man would have to die. And, if by the grace of God, there was some way that he might be able to ensure that his mother would return from New Orleans, a changed woman. A woman who was willing to cut him a fucking ounce of slack, he would make it happen. Then the world could be perfect.

Leaning back into the seat he restarted the playlist. Thinking about the possibilities that would await him when he returned from New Orleans, made him smile. He was becoming a man. He assumed this was what going to war felt like. This was his defining moment and he could feel the liberation swelling within. So he closed his eyes and fantasized about the prize; Kelly McIntyre smiling at him, naked.

Jackson Square

Terrence, Horace, Geraldine and Harold had been wandering the Quarter for the better part of an hour. Terrence, having consumed a heroic amount of absinthe floated on a green cloud from club to club listening to the music coming from each, and on more than one occasion ran back and forth across Royal Street to create his own mash up of jazz and blues.

Harold looked at Geraldine and immediately felt a bond with someone he hadn't felt since he was in high school. It was the one of getting caught, but still getting away with something. That fluttering feeling of relief when you realize your parents aren't going to be called, and the feeling of relief you share with your co-conspirators. A moment in time and singularity of emotion that for years hence you will be able to share that moment with them and still giggle.

Geraldine was amazed at how easy Harold was to talk to. He didn't interrupt, he didn't interject. She would speak and allow the words to land on him, where they would be slowly absorbed and digested. And only when he was certain that she was finished would he comment on what she had just said.

Horace watched this all unfolding and was disgusted. There was the Arab asshole making an ass out of himself, something that he excelled at; then there was the alien; and finally there was Geraldine. Horace hadn't any real designs on her. Hell he wasn't even sure if a punctuation/human union was even physically possible. Sure everyone had heard the story of Henry Miller and the ampersand, but he always chalked that up to myth. Terrence danced across Royal Street and smiled at Horace. Horace fought the urge to hit him.

"I really don't understand why the hell everyone is so God damned happy here," said Horace. "Why the hell are you so God damned happy?"

"What's your problem, man?" said Terrence.

"I thought we were going to start something here, not dance along Royal Street. I though the whole idea was to talk to Frankel and get him to shut down the Internet. That was the whole reason that we got our asses down here. That's why we crashed the convention. This was going to be some kind of glorious fucking moment where we were going to liberate the minds of the human race, unleash them from the tyranny and the bullshit. We didn't get even close to talking to him. And after that debacle I doubt if we'll get another chance."

"Well, I do know where he lives," said Harold.

"What did you say?"

"I know where he lives," said Harold. "I used to work for him."

Directions to Mr. Frankel's compound had been surprisingly easy to find. It was a simple Google search on the Internet at a bookmobile on Rampart Street. Although, none of them actually had a library card, Horace did a bit of flirting with the librarian. It really was fun to see him in his element. Rarely does one experience a punctuation mark being as appreciated as when one is with a true bibliophile. Horace also had a similar effect on owners of independent used bookstores.

"Now, I think the best course of action would be trying to break in the back door," said Horace.

"Why do we have to be all A-Team about this?" said Terrence. "Why don't we just see about knocking on the man's front door?"

"Of all the dumb fucking idiotic," said Horace. "Do you realize the kind of money that we're really talking about here? We are talking about the guy who invented the Internet. And if the rumors are true, he actually has it housed under his compound in Florida."

"The internet couldn't fit in someone's basement," said Harold. "Besides, they don't build basements in Florida."

"No, he does," said Harold. "I've seen the blueprints."

"Besides we're not talking about a regular basement. We're talking about a very, very, rich person's basement; someone who is so remarkably rich that he could, if he wanted to, buy and sell our lives. He has enough money to have us killed."

"Okay, that being said, what kind of a chance do you think we'll have trying to break in the back door?" said Terrence. "I don't know what kind of security this guy has, but I'll bet you it's impressive. So, who's to say if he is all that, that we, being the crack team that we are, would survive for ten minutes?"

"Don't do sarcasm," said Horace. "You don't do it well."

"Did it come across as snide?" said Terrence.

"No, it just clunked," said Horace.

"But, it makes a lot of sense," said Geraldine. "My bigger question is what the hell we're going to do once we find him?"

"What you think we need to all get on message?" said Horace.

"Well, yes," said Harold. "Here we are with this guy. He gives us what? Ten? Maybe fifteen minutes to make our case. So my question is, what is our case?"

"Do you want us to work up some kind of a manifesto?" said Horace.

"Yes," said Geraldine. "The Internet Counter-Revolution."

"So now we're leading a revolution?" said Harold. "I thought we just wanted to talk to the man."

"Said the guy who is leading an invasion from another planet," said Horace.

"Now that really wasn't fair," said Terrence.

Harold broke out of the bubble of conversation and looked around to find they were standing in Jackson Square Park. The number of fortunetellers had exploded in the past few days, drawn there from the prospect of spillover tourists from the Individuality™ convention. Most of them ignored Harold. He closed his eyes and began rubbing them with slight pressure. The lights exploded behind his eyelids.

The first day he had arrived in the Quarter, he quickly went from "easy mark" to "the crazy alien guy." That made him smile. The thought of all of this being due to insanity was liberating. If this were all in his head, he wouldn't have to concern himself with anyone anymore. There would be no desperate need to help people, both his and the natives of this planet. Liberation is what this was about; walking away from the pre-programmed trap of the oppressive, incessant need to belong. Mankind had already wasted billions of dollars, and hours, on self-help books, seminars, alcohol, and bowling equipment, in the hope that they might be able to find some solace in belonging. The definition of insanity is doing the same thing over and over again and expecting a different result. By this very definition it was clear that the people of this world were completely insane. Harold opened his eyes to see Geraldine standing in front of him.

"There are a handful of clichés that I could say at this moment," said Geraldine.

"It would make me very happy if you didn't," said Harold.

"You know that something has to be done," said Geraldine. "There is no way that we as a civilization can continue to go on with our obsessive narcissism. We have to stop, and begin to listen to one another."

"But, does this have to be us?" said Harold. "And does it have to be now?"

"Yes," said Geraldine. "This is the beginning of the Internet Counter-Revolution. I want you to be there."

"We just met."

"Yes, but I would very much like to continue meeting you. You aren't like everyone else. When other people talk it gets so loud sometimes in my head, but when you talk, all I ever hear is you, and, I like that. When I talk to you, I kind of get the impression that you actually listen to what I'm saying. I get the feeling that you actually want to talk to me and hear what it is that I might actually have to say."

"I'm married."

"Is that a bad thing?"

"I don't know yet."

"Do you want to go to Florida?"

"Answer wisely, that is a much bigger question that I think either of you actually understand," said the voice of the young Creole woman standing next to them.

"Who are you?" asked Harold.

"Now Harold, let's take this slowly," she said. "Would you like to know my name, or who I am? These are two very different questions." As she spoke, the other fortunetellers around Jackson Square bent an ear toward Harold, straining to hear what the young woman was going to say next. The tourists went on with their business; oblivious to the focus the locals were now giving this young woman.

"Why don't we start with your name?" said Geraldine. Horace and Terrence crowded in to hear what was happening.

"I'm Tamika Mourningwood, owner of Madam Leveaux's Voodoo Comics Emporium and Palace of Voodoo," she said.

"I'm sorry I don't believe in Voodoo," said Harold.

"That's okay, I don't believe in aliens," she said. "But, I know that something drew you here to New Orleans, and you know it, too."

"It was this amazing confluence of events which brought us all here," said Terrence.

"But, to do what?" said Tamika.

"To talk to Mr. Frankel," said Harold.

"Are you certain?" said Tamika.

"Look if you keep talking like this I am going to have to get myself another drink," said Horace. "All you're doing is sounding extra mysterious. This isn't the Matrix lady, this is the real world."

"Said the Semi-colon," said Tamika, with a broad grin.

"How do you know this?" said Terrence.

"A couple of comic books told me," said Tamika. "They sent me to tell you-"

"If she says there's a storm coming, I'm out." said Horace.

"Everything is about to change," said Tamika. "If you go to Florida, make very certain you know why you are going. There is a whole world of possibility out there. You thought about it yourself. Why not just go and be a little crazy?"

"Because, I'm not."

"Then you have my condolences," said Tamika. She smiled at Harold and slipped something into his pocket, then disappeared down Pirate's Alley.

"That kind of flipped me out a little bit," said Terrence. "Who's up for a drink?"

Harold reached into his pocket to see what Tamika had left in them and pulled out a set of car keys.

"Not now," said Harold. "We need to get going."

The next morning, HoJo was staring at the cover of Fantastic Four #48 as it hung on the wall of Madam Leveaux's Comic Emporium and Palace of Voodoo. Its faded brown cover heralded the coming of Galactus, and sported a three thousand dollar price tag. The only more expensive item in the shop was a love potion.

"Why is that one so expensive?" asked HoJo, interrupting the conversation Tamika and Ami were having.

"Which one?" said Tamika. No one wanted to have their fortunes told by Madam Tamika, but a whole lot of people needed to. This was how Ami and HoJo had found her.

"That one," said HoJo.

"It has the first appearance of the Silver Surfer," said Madam Leveaux.

"Who?" said HoJo.

"See this is what happens when fathers walk out on their families, they stunt their development," said Tamika. "You really need to get that kid to a comic book store."

"I promise you I will," lied Ami. "Do you think that there is anything that you can do to help me find my husband?"

"Sure," said Tamika.

"What is Spiderman doing on the cover of a comic called Amazing Fantasy?" said HoJo.

"Seriously?" said Tamika, as she glared at Ami. "If he keeps talking, I think I may have to charge you double."

"And exactly how much do you charge?"

"That depends on how quickly you want the information," said Tamika. "I can check his credit card charges, his Individuality™ page, and see if his *find my phone* app is working. I check all of that and send you back to your bed and breakfast in the Quarter to cool off for the night. I'll give you the results first thing in the morning, and it will only cost you two fifty. Or, I could give you this, and it will cost you two thousand dollars." Tamika placed a small black box on the table.

"What is that?" said Ami.

"Tracking device for the anti theft system I had installed on my car last week," said Tamika.

"Why would I want that?"

"It's the same car your husband stole last night," said Tamika. "Of course, stole is really rather a strong way to put it. If I really thought he stole it, I could just turn this over to the police and let them find him."

"Please, don't," said Ami.

"Why?" said Tamika. "What is he to you other than a complication?"

"An embarrassment," said HoJo.

"Take me up on the cheaper offer," said Tamika. "Go back to your room and sleep on it. If you still want it tomorrow I sell it to you for a grand."

"You want me to sleep on it?" said Ami. "You want to see how badly I need this, kind of like a cooling down period for selling someone a gun."

"Nothing that noble," said Madam Leveaux. "This is pure extortion."

Ami resisted the urge to slap her. She knew that this supposed mystic was just trying to get the better of her. Hell, she freely admitted to it. But, it didn't make resisting the urge to smack her any less enticing.

"What the hell is a JSA?" interrupted HoJo.

"HoJo," snapped Ami. "Shut the hell up."

Ami pulled out her credit card, and Madam Leveaux disappeared into a back room.

HoJo peered at the breasts on one of the comic book covers.

"He is in Florida," said Tamika, as she returned handing Ami the box. "I need to talk to your son."

"Why?" said Ami.

"I need to talk to your son."

"If this has something to do with Harold I want to know," said Ami.

"This all has something to do with Harold. You wouldn't be here if it weren't for Harold. You would still be sitting in Chicago trying to sell over priced homes to people who neither want nor need them. You would be part of the problem."

"And, now you're going to try to tell me that now, with Harold's help, I can become part of the solution?"

"No, you're a waste of space, but I was hoping that if I could have a word with your son, I might just be able to send him down a path where he won't become like you."

"You think it's better to believe you're a damned alien."

"I think it's better to believe in something. If you allow me to talk to him for a moment, you can be on your way with my blessing. Otherwise, you can fuck off."

Ami slowly got to her feet and walked out.

"You should think about buying a magazine," said Tamika.

"What?" sputtered HoJo.

"You need to get a tittie mag, and jack off. Hard. You're so pent up you're going to do something stupid."

"I don't need to listen to you," said HoJo. "I bet that's what you say to all teenage boys. It must be quite a revelation that a teenage boy might just be sexually frustrated. Tell me, what did you guess about my mother? That she might be lonely and underappreciated as a middle-aged woman who is estranged from her insane husband?"

"Boy, there is frustrated, and then there is you. You need to drain that thing quick. Or, something really very frightening is going to happen. Do you understand me?"

HoJo backed toward the door.

"Take this," she said handing him a map, and a nudie mag. "The map is for your mother, the mag for you. It's on the house, just please do something, before someone gets hurt."

Sawgrass Breeze

All men, when they look in the mirror, never see the individual that is reflected. Instead, all men see some distorted version of their thirteen-year-old self. It is how one deals with this thirteen year old, which determines how the person presents himself. If they come to terms with their thirteen-year-old, you will usually find a man who may be described as a slight slacker, one who is embracing the geekier side of who he is. If, however, the individual lives in denial, they will try almost anything to cover up their imagined failings.

Mr. Frankel was desperately ashamed of his inner thirteen-year-old. This is what led to his subsequent obsession with his favorite hobbies, masturbation and pornography. Had Mr. Frankel been more at ease with his inner thirteen-year-old, he would have recognized masturbation to be a very normal and healthy activity. But, his denial of it, fed his obsession with it. This obsession led him to invent the Internet. Many people assume that the Internet was invented as a way to quickly send messages from one computer to another, and has now grown to such proportions to be the world's largest repository for knowledge on the face of the planet. This is false. The Internet is now, and always has been, a highly efficient way for people to anonymously share vast amounts of pornography. Mr. Frankel built the Internet and placed it in the basement of his compound in Florida, so that no one would know his dirty little secret.

Mr. Frankel's favorite pornographic images were modern reproductions of classic pin up art. He preferred the models to be redheads, and shaved. He also, on occasion, enjoyed auto asphyxiation. It had been a recent collection of photos that recreated an early Betty Page photo shoot with a nude redhead, shown as a slide show on his new one hundred and fifty inch 3-D television, that he was watching when he lost his footing.

Most days there would be a discreet gentleman, named Jenkins who would attend to the possibility of Mr. Frankel actually killing himself. Unfortunately, for Mr. Frankel he had absentmindedly fired Jenkins, due to an unrelated incident. Jenkins had immediately left the compound and contacted his brother in law, who worked for a publishing house, about the possibility of a book deal. The tell-all book regarding Mr. Frankel would make the discreet gentleman a very rich man. Mr. Frankel had been too drunk, as well as too excited, to actually bother to check that Jenkins would be there to assist him if anything went wrong.

This was how Harold, Geraldine, Horace and Terrence found Mr. Frankel; hanging naked in front of a one hundred and fifty inch 3-D television set showing images of a naked redhead in various bizarre poses.

"Oh, my," said Geraldine.

"Fuck," said Horace.

"Do you think he's dead?" said Terrence.

"I don't know," said Harold. "I've never actually seen a dead body."

"Why don't you see if he has a pulse?" said Terrence.

"Why don't you see if he has a pulse!" said Harold. "You're the one who worked in a hospital."

"So, you have a kid," said Terrence.

"What does that have to do with anything?" said Harold.

"Well you've had to change diapers and stuff like that," said Terrence.

"What the hell does a diaper have to do with a dead body?" said Harold.

"A suspected dead body, we can't be sure until we actually find out," said Terrence. "For all we know he still is clinging to life right now."

"Shouldn't we cut him down then?" said Harold.

"Wouldn't that be interfering with the crime scene?" said Terrence. "I remember once doing a show and everyone was all about preserving the integrity of the crime scene. Everyone was screaming not to touch anything; that if your skin cells or your hair ended up on the body they wouldn't be able to find the actual killer. Or worse it would all end up pointing to you."

"Then why was it you wanted me to touch the body?"

"That was the other thing that they kept doing in the show, they would make certain that the bodies were dead."

"So they would all stand around screaming that no one should touch the bodies, and then someone would have to go and actually check to see if the body was actually dead," said Horace. "That makes absolutely no fucking sense; you do realize this don't you?"

"That was what I kept telling them on the set, but they just didn't want to hear any of it, they just weren't paying any attention to me," said Terrence.

"Calm down," said Harold. "We didn't do anything wrong here, so all we really need to do is walk away, right?"

"Walk away?" said Terrence.

"Well no one knows that we're actually here do they?" said Harold. "Why don't we just leave?"

"We can't," said Geraldine.

"She's right," said Horace. "We can't."

"Why?" said Terrence.

"We've come this far for one very beautiful reason, to take down the Internet, if only for a couple of days, do you realize what could happen over those days, once the panic subsides?" said Horace. "People will actually start communicating with one another again. They will look at each other in the eye and realize that in there is another human being, not just some kid gaming with me a world away, but an actual person right there, with hopes dreams and desires, that can't fit within 140 characters. At this moment my friends, we stand at the precipice of a remarkable moment in history. We can, right here, right now, bring about the Internet counter-revolution, and you want to walk away from that, Mr. Alien? The whole damned reason you're here, to hopefully get people to start thinking for themselves? I'm not going anywhere. I'm going to find out where the Individuality™ servers are and shut them down."

"That was beautiful," said Geraldine.

"They're in the basement," said Harold.

"How do you know that the servers are in the basement?" said Terrence.

"I was Mr. Frankel's office manager when he was building the compound," said Harold. "I know he put them down there."

"Then why didn't you say something?" said Horace.

"About what?" said Harold.

"About the servers," said Horace. "If we knew where they were, then why the hell would we need him? At this point who cares if he's dead or not?"

"I might care," said Harold. "He was always really nice to me. Understandably, I was brainwashed at the time, but he still seemed very nice."

"Fine we can mourn him later," said Horace. "Cut him down and we'll go look at those servers."

The faux wood paneling in the doublewide made it nearly impossible to hang anything on the walls. Nails would bend, or worse, puncture the vinyl siding of the doublewide, allowing even more of the rain and humidity in. The lack of insulation for the double wide surprisingly never caused it to be cold, but nearly impossible to keep cool. Even in the winter the occupants of the offices housed in the doublewide would be forced to run the loud air conditioners.

The doublewide itself precariously bridged a drainage ditch, which ran next to a swamp, possibly the least desirable piece of real estate in the entire gated community of Sawgrass Breeze. This was by design. No one in the homeowners association was going to give the offices for the security guards a prime piece of Florida real estate overlooking the Atlantic. No, instead they got a secluded piece of property that bordered on a swamp. This was something that never much bothered Sheriff Bobby.

The term "Sheriff" was something he had negotiated into his contract as the head of security for Sawgrass Breeze. This wasn't any delusion of grandeur, Sheriff Bobby knew that he was only a step or two above a mall cop, but he brought a kind of folksy charm to the community of Sawgrass Breeze. Sheriff Bobby likened himself to an Andy Griffith for the über-wealthy who populated the vast mansions and compounds located on the grounds. He knew the homeowners well, and understood that there was always leeway when it came to any dispute; which, when the dispute was between homeowners, was something that could usually be handled with both sides sitting down and having a cappuccino. If it needed to be escalated, it would usually be something to do with some bored rich kid, and the homeowners association could easily handle it with a fine and a phone call.

Even the occasional domestic accident could be tastefully taken care of without the intrusion of the actual authorities. The homeowners didn't want them in, and neither did Sheriff Bobby. He liked the little niche in the world he had carved out for himself. He sat at his desk in the back of the doublewide with his feet up on his desk and his hat pulled low across his eyes. He had even considered taking up the banjo to help him project even more of a folksy charm.

"Sheriff," said Mary. Mary had been working as the head dispatcher for the security office for the past seven years. He made certain that no one ever referred to her as a secretary.

"Yes, Mary," he said, trying to sound like she had woken him from a nap.

"I just had the damnedest call from David," said Mary.

"So what else is new?" said the Sheriff. David was one of the newly hired members of the security force. He approached his job with an unparalleled zeal and exuberance, which was starting to become annoying.

"He says that someone's broken into Mr. Frankel's place," said Mary.

"Damnit," said Sheriff Bobby, as he slowly rose to his feet. "If David is spying on one of Mr. Frankel's parties again, there'll be hell to pay."

"I don't think so," said Mary. "David said he thought he saw an Arab and some kind of a punctuation mark."

"A what?"

"An Arab and a punctuation mark," said Mary. "Do you want me to get him on the phone, Sheriff?"

"No, I had better get down there before he ends up doing something stupid," he said.

"You gonna take one of the carts?"

"Might as well."

Sheriff Bobby had never been a fan of the golf carts. The homeowners association had purchased them for the express purpose of allowing the security personnel to make their way across the vast estates, without causing an increase in emissions. They did have flashing red and blue lights on the top, but humming along, at a top speed of slightly faster than walking, made him feel like a douche bag.

David loved the golf carts. David was a douche bag.

Sheriff Bobby didn't have the slightest idea what Mr. Frankel actually did to make his millions. To be honest, he had little to no idea what most of the people who lived in Sawgrass Breeze did to amass their fortunes. Unless there was an emergency, he rarely checked out the profiles of the residents. He felt they paid for a certain level of privacy and security, and he was ready to ensure they had it, not root around in their private files.

David, however, felt strongly that knowledge was power, and there was a level of confidentiality, but there was also the need for him to be able to do his job, and do it well. David took a good deal of pride in his job. Sometimes more than was actually required of him.

The golf cart bounced up the trail behind the Frankel compound. Sheriff Bobby could see that David was lying on his stomach near the top of the hill.

"David, damnit!" said Sheriff Bobby. "What have I told you about spying on folks?"

"Shush!" admonished David. If there was one thing that Sheriff Bobby couldn't stand, it was being shushed. But, he also knew that David knew he didn't like it, so he must think there was something serious going on at the Frankel estate.

For a douche bag he means well, thought Sheriff Bobby as he hiked up the small rise.

"This had better be good," whispered Sheriff Bobby.

David didn't say a word, he simply handed the binoculars to him. Reluctantly, Sheriff Bobby looked through them.

"I'll admit it does look a little strange," said Sheriff Bobby. "I see an Arab, some kind of a punctuation mark, and a Caucasian couple, but I don't see what was making you so nuts, David. Mr. Frankel has held a few parties in his time, with some strange folks."

"Third window, from northwest corner," whispered David.

Sheriff Bobby looked through the binoculars at the window. It took a moment for his brain to register that he was seeing, a pair of feet swinging into and then out of view. It took him even longer to realize that the feet probably belonged to Mr. Frankel. And an even longer moment to understand that with the way that the body was swinging that Mr. Frankel was probably hanging by his neck.

"Well, shit," said Sheriff Bobby. "I guess we'd better get on over there and see what the hell is going on."

"What the hell?" said David. "Am I the only one he who can see that there is a damned Arab over there!? You know the protocol when residents end up dead."

"Yes, but if Mr. Frankel inadvertently killed himself while trying to jack off, I don't want to have a whole bunch of federal authorities finding his bloated body, especially if he was doing something extra stupid."

"Article sixty two, subsection B of the homeowners association bylaws is very explicit."

"Look all I'm saying is that I don't want us to go off half cocked," said Sheriff Bobby, trying to sound calm. "Let me have Mary pull his file, and then we can go from there."

"You just want to go on up and knock on the damned door? What the hell is wrong with you? You brain dead hick."

"Why don't we all just take a long deep breath here, before we say some things we don't mean here," said Sheriff Bobby.

David and Sheriff Bobby both inhaled deeply through their noses and out through their mouths; just like they were taught at the conflict resolution seminar last month.

"David, I need you to listen to me very carefully," continued Sheriff Bobby. "I need to head back to the doublewide; there are a few things I need to check. I need you to keep the house under surveillance."

"Do you want me to get a closer look?"

"No I just want you to sit tight, do you understand?"

David nodded as Sheriff Bobby walked back to the golf cart. He tried to not mutter, "Fuck" repeatedly as he spun around on the service road and headed back to the doublewide. But, it was all that he could say.

Mary had seen Sheriff Bobby loose his cool maybe four times in the past 20 years they had worked with each other. He was always the guy you wanted in a crisis. Nice and level headed. He was always the one in the room everyone looked to for guidance. When he walked in muttering the word "Fuck" over and over again, she knew there was something serious going on.

Mary quietly brought the thin folder over for Sheriff Bobby. She was surprised at how thin the folder was. One of the terms of becoming a homeowner in Sawgrass Breeze was a confidential folder to be opened in the event of a homeowner's death. Mary and Sheriff Bobby had to open two of confidential folders in their years at Sawgrass Breeze. Inside might be copies of a will, the contact number of their lawyers and next of kin, or special instruction on how the body should, or should not be found. There had been the 259-pound former Senator that they had to remove from the lavender taffeta evening gown and ball gag. Then there had been the former supermodel that requested the refrigerator be stocked, so no one would think she had died due to her eating disorder.

Sheriff Bobby opened the folder to find a lone sheet of loose-leaf paper with a phone number on it.

"Well shit," said Sheriff Bobby. "This sure as hell looks cryptic."

"Are you gonna call it," said Mary.

"Hell, Mary, of course I'm going to call it."

"You want me to dial it for you?" said Mary. "I know you probably could, but your hands are shaking something fierce, Sheriff."

"Damnit Mary, he hung himself, naked."

"Do you think it might have been some kind of accident?"

"Don't know, yet. It looked like there were other folks there. I don't know if it was one of his parties gone wrong, or something worse? But, one of them was an Arab."

"Well why don't we see about calling that number," she said, as she picked up the handset.

"I'm scared, Mary."

"Now Sheriff, we've done this before, and unfortunately we'll be doing this again, but that is no reason to lose your nerve."

"I know Mary, but this time it just feels different."

"Well, this is the first time it has been Mr. Frankel."

That wasn't what Sheriff Bobby meant, she knew it wasn't what Sheriff Bobby meant, but at the same time she knew if she let her concern show, it might just cause him to begin to break down.

"Hello," said the voice on the other end of the phone.

"Please hold," said Mary, as she held the phone out to Sheriff Bobby.

"Sheriff Bobby here," he said into the phone. "To whom am I speaking?"

"Are you certain that Mr. Frankel is dead?" said the voice on the other line.

"Pretty sure."

"Is the house secure?"

"No there are people in it, and I think one of them might be an Arab. Are you going to tell me who the hell you are?"

"We will have our people there on the ground in forty five minutes. Please wait for further instructions until our field personnel have arrived."

Endings

The black semi pulling the extra long black trailer was preceded by a black bus, a pair of black SUVs and three black motorcycles with sirens and flashing lights. The guards at the front gate of Sawgrass Breeze didn't hesitate to call Sheriff Bobby when they had arrived. Sheriff Bobby didn't hesitate to head to the gate to meet them. As he did, he said a tiny prayer under his breath that this wouldn't end up being the end of his career with Sawgrass Breeze.

"I was wondering if I might be able to talk to whoever is in charge?" said Sheriff Bobby to one of the men on the motorcycles.

"Why that would be you, Sheriff Bobby!" said the man in the black suit who was exiting the black bus and walking toward Sheriff Bobby. "Why, we aren't even officially supposed to be here. We are only here to help you, Sheriff Bobby. And help you as subtly as we can."

"Look, unless you boys can tell me who the hell you are I'm not going to be able to let you in. Do you understand?"

"Of course we do," said the man in black. "You are just trying to do your job to the best of your ability, and not only do we understand, but we also respect that. However, Sheriff Bobby, you called us. We're just here to help you with the issue at Mr. Frankel's house. Now the longer you leave us on this side of the gate not only will the situation inside the compound get worse, but how long will it take for the other residents to begin to wonder why there is a caravan outside of their gated community? After that, how long before the television cameras begin showing up?"

Sheriff Bobby knew that this was going to somehow lead to the end of his career. But, he also knew that how he ended it would be up to him. Would he be able to look the homeowners association in the face and say that he had done everything he could to not only contain, but to also eliminate the danger to them? Say what you will about his hokey charm, Sheriff Bobby was a man who was firmly rooted in his sense of duty. He found himself explaining to the guard to let the trucks through, and to put Sawgrass Breeze on lockdown until the issue had been resolved. Then at the invitation of the man in black, he was invited onto the bus. He might as well have been invited onto an alien ship.

The large screens showed images of the Frankel compound, both inside and out. There were also blueprints showing weak points as well as the fallout shelter and a large basement.

"Thank you Sheriff Bobby," said the man in black. "If I were here in any kind of official capacity, I would be certain to make a comment about how helpful you have been."

"Hypothetically speaking then, I guess I would say thank you," said Sheriff Bobby.

"Hypothetically speaking, that is really quite amusing. Do you know what Mr. Frankel did to make his fortune?"

"I usually don't like to pry, but I think it had something to do with that website, Individuality™. Not that I ever used it, but my assistant Mary does; helps her keep up with her kids."

"That is a quaint supposition, but in reality, Mr. Frankel actually invented the Internet, and has it housed in the basement of his compound."

"So he has a couple of servers..."

"No, Sheriff Bobby he has the entire Internet housed in his basement."

"But, the Internet is too big for that."

"Sheriff Bobby, forgive me, I didn't take you for a computer scientist; just a dumb hick in a rent a cop uniform."

"I'm not a computer expert."

"So, when I ask you how big is the actual Internet, you would most likely say?"

"I don't really know."

"As do most people. The fact of the matter is Mr. Frankel invented the Internet as an efficient way for he and his colleagues to share things."

"I thought the Internet was a resource?"

"Yes for the quick distribution of a phenomenal amount of pornography. Everything else was just to make it seem acceptable to the rest of society that didn't want an instrument of degradation and smut into your home."

"It sounds to me like you didn't much like the idea."

"Most of us didn't."

"Then why didn't you stop it?"

"By the time we realized what was going on, it had become such an integral part of most people's lives that there was no easy way to get them to disconnect. Every time we tried, or even tried to talk Mr. Frankel into allowing us to remove the filth and place it on a separate server, either there would be protests, or he would end up objecting so vehemently that he threatened to pull the plug on the whole net. But, by now, do you realize the volume of money that changes hands via the Internet?"

"No."

"On a slow day, one of the biggest money transfer sites can hit over two hundred thousand transactions. Could you imagine what would happen to the economy as a whole if we were to just turn it off?"

"I think that it might be kind of bad."

"I think that would be kind of an understatement," said the man in black. "You mentioned that the compound has been compromised."

"David says he thinks one of them might be Arab," said Sheriff Bobby.

"Well, hopefully we will be able to work this to all of our advantage here, Sheriff Bobby. There is a strong possibility that you might just be able to come out the other side of this with a healthy raise from the homeowners association, but you are going to have to follow my instructions perfectly, do you understand me?"

"Yes, I just want this issue to be over with."

"Don't worry, Sheriff. By tonight this should be all over," said the man in black, as the bus came to a halt. Outside a flurry of activity commenced, as preparations were made to secure the compound.

"Well," continued the man in black. "Shall we go see what is going on?"

Exiting the bus, Sheriff Bobby was shocked to see how the calm exterior of the Frankel Compound had been transformed. It now appeared to be a home under siege. Snipers took aim at the house; one man in uniform was ushering David over to the man in black and Sheriff Bobby.

"Sir, they still appear to be inside the compound, but I fear they've spotted us," said David.

"Of, course they have," said the man in black. "How are we supposed to begin negotiations if they don't know we're here?"

"Negotiations?" said Sheriff Bobby.

"Here," said the man in black, as he handed a cell phone to the Sheriff. "Let's make first contact and go from there."

"Shouldn't you be doing that?" said Sheriff Bobby.

"We're not really even here," said the man in black.

Sheriff Bobby put the cell phone to his ear. He sat and listened to the phone continue to ring.

"It's just ringing," he said.

"Maybe we should storm the house," said David.

"Calm down, son," said Sheriff Bobby. "There is a process to all of this."

"Well put, Sheriff," said the man in black, as a man off the bus handed him a megaphone. "Answer the phone!" he screamed into it.

"Who the hell lets the phone ring that many times?" said the voice on the other end of the line.

"To whom am I speaking?" said Sheriff Bobby.

"Me," said the voice. "Who the hell are you? Doesn't this weirdo have voice mail? What kind of a person doesn't have voice mail?"

"My name is Sheriff Bobby," he said. "Am I speaking to the Arab or the punctuation mark?"

"Semi colon," said the voice.

"Are you the one that comes between the numbers on a clock or the other one?" said Sheriff Bobby.

"The other one."

"Should I just call you Semi colon, or do you have a name?"

"I do, but I'm not quite certain I should give it to you."

"What should I call you then?"

"You can call me, Al."

"Alright, Al. Is Mr. Frankel okay?"

"No he's dead."

"He was dead when we got here," said a second voice.

"Who said that?" said Sheriff Bobby.

"I did," said the second voice. "I'm Terrence."

"You dumb drunk asshole," said the first voice.

"Don't call me an asshole, Horace."

"Al?" said Sheriff Bobby. "Is Horace your real name?"

"Of course it is," said Terrence. "Go ahead, tell him, Horace."

"Of all the dumb ass things to do," said Horace. "All we want to do is shut down the Internet. Just for a little while."

"Can you tell me if there is anyone else in the compound with you?" said Sheriff Bobby.

"Yes, Harold Winestock, he's from Chicago," said Terrence. "And Geraldine, but I don't know where she's from."

"Terrence, can I ask you one more quick question," said Sheriff Bobby.

"Sure, but Horace is getting a little angry with me, so I'm going to have to hang up soon."

"Before you do, can you tell me if you're the Arab person in the house?"

"I'm from Detroit," said Terrence as the line went dead.

The man in black took the phone from Sheriff Bobby, and gave him a pat on the back.

"You've done very well, however you need to understand that since you were talking to a hostile punctuation mark and an Arab, you have to take it all with a grain of salt," said the man in black. "That being said, you've given us a great deal to work with."

The cell phone in Sheriff Bobby's hand began to ring. He thought about not answering it. This was the tipping point, where things spiral out of control. Sheriff Bobby tried to hand it to the man in black. If the man in black had taken the phone at that moment, he could have walked away. The man in black just stared at the cell phone. Sheriff Bobby could just not answer the phone.

"Hello?" he said answering it.

"Sheriff?" said Mary's voice on the other end. "I've got a woman at the front gate with her son. She says he's here to look for her husband. I know you're dealing with an awful lot right now, but she just won't take no for an answer."

"Well, who is she and who is her husband?"

"She says her name is Ami Winestock, and her husband's name is Harold Winestock."

Sheriff Bobby dropped the phone. It hit the asphalt hard; picking it up he saw that the crack ran down the length of the screen, and ran directly over the end call icon. He tried to push it to end the call, but all he could hear Mary's voice calling to him from the tiny speaker.

Ami and HoJo were met at the gates by Sheriff Bobby and the man in black.

"I'm sorry," said Ami. "But, a crazy black lady gave me this to track my husband. He has been making an ass out of himself lately. To be perfectly honest, I really think the real reason I'm here might have something more to do with me."

"If you don't say something she might actually begin to ramble," said HoJo. "You wouldn't like her when she rambles, it can get a little crazy."

"You're husband may have killed someone," said Sheriff Bobby.

"Anyone important?" said Ami.

"The inventor of the Internet," said the man in black.

"Fuck," said HoJo.

"Sheriff Bobby has already begun negotiations," said the man in black.

"Has he made any demands?" said Ami. "Has he asked to speak with me?"

"They want to shut down the Internet," said Sheriff Bobby.

"Fuck," said HoJo.

"Has he asked for anything?" said Ami.

"No, so far I've only talked to the semi colon," said Sheriff Bobby.

"No one can just shut down the Internet," said HoJo

"The Internet is housed in Mr. Frankel's basement," said the man in black.

They both paused for the expletive, which they had begun to expect from HoJo, to find that he was no longer with them. He had entered the gated community and was beginning to walk toward Mr. Frankel's estate.

"HoJo!" screamed Ami.

"Let him go for a walk, he'll be alright," said the man in black.

"But, what about all the snipers?" said Sheriff Bobby.

"Remember Sheriff, we're not really here."

HoJo was walking through every action movie he had ever seen in his short thirteen years. There were people with guns running past him, setting up barriers and securing the area. Through this HoJo walked with a bizarre confidence and joy. He saw snipers on roofs with rifles, and another setting up on the hood of a van. He found it strange that he was allowed such access. He looked over the shoulder of people who were working, lining up shots. His mother and the man in black were still talking. HoJo was done with talking; he had to find some way to make Harold seem so perfectly deplorable, that his inevitable death would be forgivable.

"I really don't think that going out there is really the best of ideas," said Terrence.

"I think I have to agree with the mad Arab here," said Horace.

"Look, if they think that we're some kind of terrorist group, then we'll be written off as a bunch of lunatics," said Harold.

"Said the guy who claims to be an alien," said Horace. "I don't know why the hell anyone would think that?"

"I'll be right out front," said Harold. "It will give you time to shut down the servers safely."

Geraldine turned to Harold and smiled.

"This is where I should be saying something moderately inspiring," said Geraldine. "Or maybe even a little cliché."

"I'm glad you didn't," said Harold.

"You know they'll never believe us about Mr. Frankel's death," said Horace.

"But, maybe if I stall, you can shut down the servers," said Harold.

He walked out the front door of the house.

All of the officers were on their toes. The word had gone around that one of the hostage takers actually wanted to speak to the negotiator, and wanted to have the press present when he did it. A few of the S.W.A.T. detail were sent to find suits and cameras to pretend to be the local media. Everything looked prepared, as the pudgy guy came walking out the front door of the house.

"Please take three large steps forward," said Sheriff Bobby.

The pudgy guy complied.

"You wife is here," he continued. "Would you like to speak to her?"

"Not particularly," said the pudgy guy.

"Why are you here?"

"We wanted to shut down the Internet," said the pudgy guy. "Not permanently. Just for a little while. Just so everyone would take a minute and actually listen to what was going on around him or her, which I'll be honest with you, is something that can get a bit scary. But, once you start doing it, it can be really rather remarkable."

"What are your demands?" said the negotiator.

"We don't really have any. We just wanted to take a minute before everything goes crazy, to explain what happened."

"Why do you think everything is going to go crazy?"

"Because, Mr. Frankel is dead."

"Why did you kill him, and are there any other hostages in the estate?"

"We didn't kill him, it appears to have been a mistake."

It had been a nacho that had caused the stroke that set Harold on his path to his truth. It was also a nacho that had caused the premature death of the S.W.A.T. sniper on the roof of the van. HoJo nearly tripped over the dead body, and climbed up to the roof of the van to find the abandoned rifle. If this were a movie, a shiny bit would have caused a glint of sun to bounce off it. But, the rifle sat there on top of the van, inviting HoJo. Looking through the high power scope on the top of the rifle he could see the front door of the Frankel estate.

The door opened and his father emerged. He began speaking. But, HoJo was too far away to make out what he was saying. HoJo reached his hand closer to the trigger. The metal was cold against his hand, almost soothing in the humidity of the day.

Pop!

That was the only noise that it made; a spot of red spread across Harold's shirt.

HoJo, tried to feel remorseful, he tried to feel anything. He climbed down from the top of the van.

"Did you see that?" said Horace.

"Where's Geraldine?" said Terrence.

The basement was cool; the fans from the servers whirred loudly. Geraldine stepped into the dust free room. Just the static and dust on her blouse could have, inadvertently caused the whole system to collapse. Of course since that was exactly what Geraldine wanted, it didn't. She eyed the long cords that went deep into the wall. They didn't even look like regular plugs, they looked like industrial cables. This was due to the fact that they were industrial cables, and not regular plugs. Geraldine didn't know where to start. Then there was silence. Something had changed. There was at this very moment something fundamentally different about the universe. Her mind tried to put it into context. It was something so huge that was now missing that she could no longer hear. Horace was behind her screaming. But, she heard nothing. For the first time in her life there was silence. She began laughing and weeping at the same moment. The two opposing emotional cathartic responses threw her body into intense convulsions. The force of the convulsions tipped the first server, it slammed into the next, and like a series of dominoes the Internet died.

There are very few people who honestly forget where they were the day the Internet died. Most people thought that it would enable some kind of huge cataclysm. But, in reality, it was nothing more worrying than one's television set going out. Once it was established that the issue was neither with individual service providers, nor IT departments, everyone relaxed a little. For many it was really rather entertaining that they could not be reached by their office via e-mail. People actually had to use the phone; where before an e-mail could be sent with a slight feel of anonymity, now people had to actually speak to each other. Instead of the ten or twenty small requests that were shot off across the Internet via e-mail, people had to actually compile all of these requests into one phone call. Once they were, these seemingly small requests actually did seem like one really very large one. By then many people felt that if they just hunkered down and did their job, they wouldn't need to ask for multiple favors. This enabled high performers to actually do their job in relative peace. The economy prospered. Social interactions became the norm. Work life balance was achieved.

HoJo and Ami were interrogated. After six hours it became a much more logical idea to forget about the whole incident, instead of filling out the necessary paperwork for leaving a loaded sniper rifle unattended. HoJo tried his best to look remorseful. Ami tried to remain in control.

Geraldine openly wept. When any one tried to speak to her she would simply stare blankly and then explode in another round of laughing and crying.

The Arab and the Semi colon were never found, and considered to be an urban legend. But, some people say that wherever horrible social stereotypes prosper, or bad grammar, they will be there. And someday they will return, when humanity reaches their darkest hour. Others say that there was a tunnel out back of the Frankel estate, which was occasionally used for dead hooker disposal, which they snuck out, returned to New Orleans, and are still drinking Absinthe heavily.

15297421R00132

Made in the USA
Charleston, SC
27 October 2012